with that smudge of flour on your nose and your hair curling up tightly from the heat of the oven," he murmured, tilting her chin so that she met his eyes.

"You're only saying that because you're a man and the way to your heart is through your stomach," she laughed. Leaning back just far enough to deny him a taste of her lips, she knew she'd give in to him in a moment. "I'd advise you to be careful, or you'll have flour all over your front," she added. "Everyone will know why you dragged me out here."

Alex grinned. He was looking inordinately pleased with her for teasing him. "They know anyway," he said.

Then, one hand tangling in the curls at her nape, he proceeded to go after what he wanted.

Dear Reader,

Welcome to Silhouette! Our goal is to give you hours of unbeatable reading pleasure, and we hope you'll enjoy each month's six new Silhouette Desires. These sensual, provocative love stories are both believable and compelling—sometimes they're poignant, sometimes humorous, but always enjoyable.

Indulge yourself. Experience all the passion and excitement of falling in love along with our heroine as she meets the irresistible man of her dreams and together they overcome all obstacles in the path to a happy ending.

If this is your first Desire, I hope it'll be the first of many. If you're already a Silhouette Desire reader, thanks for your support! Look for some of your favorite authors in the coming months: Stephanie James, Diana Palmer, Dixie Browning, Ann Major and Doreen Owens Malek, to name just a few.

Happy reading!

Isabel Swift
Senior Editor

SDRL-7/85

SUZANNE CAREY
Confess to Apollo

Silhouette Desire

Published by Silhouette Books New York

America's Publisher of Contemporary Romance

SILHOUETTE BOOKS
300 E. 42nd St., New York, N.Y. 10017

ISBN: 0-373-05268-5

First Silhouette Books printing March 1986

America's Publisher of Contemporary Romance

Printed in the U.S.A.

SUZANNE CAREY,

a reporter by training, a romance writer by choice, likes to research her stories carefully and write about the places and people she knows best. For this reason, her books have a real-life quality that intrigues readers as much as it touches their hearts.

One

"I assume you're aware of the Tarpon Springs problem."

Zoe Walker stared at her boss, Florida governor Jim Haverhill. Oh, please, she thought, anything but that. Unbidden, images of the predominantly Greek sponge-fishing port where she'd spent the first nine years of her childhood crowded into her memory.

Of course she'd read about the recent flap there concerning the former sponge exchange, a once-busy marketplace used by the town's sponge fishermen that was now crumbling and abandoned.

Several months earlier, Kalandris Enterprises—known throughout the state as a wealthy contracting and boat-building firm—had purchased the property. Stavros Kalandris, the company president, had announced plans to convert the former market into a stylish, ethnic shopping plaza—over the protest of conservative elements in the Greek community.

Tempers had flared, and those who wanted to restore the exchange as a historic landmark had appealed to the state. Though the governor seemed disposed to help them, Zoe had no particular sympathy for either side. The truth was, she never wanted to hear about Tarpon Springs again.

"I'd rather pass on this assignment, if you don't mind," she managed finally, knowing she'd probably have to elaborate.

The bushy gray brows that always characterized Jim Haverhill in political cartoons elevated slightly. "I expect you have your reasons," he replied.

Seated across from him in the shapely red sweater and trim man-tailored skirt she had chosen for this crisp December day, Zoe was a study in conflicting emotions.

Distractedly she raked the fingers of one tanned, slender hand through short bronze-gold curls. How could she possibly tell Jim just what that small, old-fashioned town beside the Gulf of Mexico symbolized to her? How could she share memories of the *Yaya*, her grandmother, or make any outsider understand what had happened there?

Even now, so many years afterward, she felt a rush of anger that made the topic a difficult one to broach. Yet Jim was more friend and mentor than employer, and she owed him an explanation.

"Maybe you didn't know..." she began, choosing her words with care. "I was born there. But my mother wasn't Greek and she was always treated as an outsider...especially by my grandmother. We moved away after my father died."

The governor regarded her thoughtfully as he tamped down a pipeful of tobacco. "I'm sorry to hear your childhood memories aren't completely happy ones," he said. "But after the way you handled things in Miami last month..."

Zoe, who had helped to work out a tricky compromise between two warring constituencies in Miami's Spanish-speaking community, didn't reply. She wasn't averse to the compliment, but neither did she plan to let it change her mind.

"Anyhow," her boss continued after a moment, "Blaine tells me you speak the language."

Something wary flickered in Zoe's large brown eyes at the mention of her ex-husband, state legislator Blaine Walker. She might still prefer his surname to the Greek one that was hers by birth, but their recent divorce in the wake of his philandering had been a low point in her life. She wasn't pleased to learn he'd been discussing her behind her back.

"Well, he ought to know better," she replied, keeping her composure. "I don't remember any Greek...just a few isolated phrases. Blaine didn't recommend me for this job, by any chance?"

Jim shrugged. "What if he did? As it happens, he read my mind. The truth is, we need somebody down there right away. We can't fish or cut bait about that property until the special session of the legislature next month. In the meantime, I don't want Stavros Kalandris and his sons taking a wrecking ball to the site. There won't be much history to preserve if they transform it into a pile of rubble."

Zoe gave an almost imperceptible sigh. Whenever Jim's voice took on that quietly determined note, he usually got his way. She loved her job as his special assistant and political troubleshooter. If she wanted to keep it, she supposed, she'd have to do as he wished.

Unfortunately the issue of returning to the place where she'd been born really wasn't a casual one with her. The very thought of it had given her a shaky, faintly light-headed feeling.

"What's Blaine's ax to grind in all this, anyway?" she asked, feeling somewhat cornered and saying the first thing that came into her head.

If Jim thought she should get on with her life and forget her former mate and his blond, Anglo-Saxon good looks, he didn't say so. "I guess you know he's going to run for Congress in the fall," he reminded her. "Tarpon Springs will be in his district."

After her four-year marriage to Blaine, Zoe was hardly politically naive. As she packed an overnight bag Saturday evening in the Tallahassee apartment she shared with law clerk Carole Foster, she realized her boss had reasons of his own for wanting an amicable settlement to the sponge-market question. Nearing the end of his second term as governor, he planned to be on the November ticket in a bid for the U.S. Senate. She herself hoped to accompany him to Washington after the election.

Anyone who knew the political geography of the state knew that Pinellas County, where Tarpon Springs was situated, would be a key area for any statewide candidate. And it didn't matter that the Greek fishing port where she had agreed to represent Jim Haverhill's interests was still essentially a small town. During the course of her assignment, she might very well come face-to-face with some of her Spritos relatives—even with the *Yaya* herself.

Or with the kind of man Jim was teasing me about, she added, pushing thoughts of her grandmother aside as she tucked favorite jeans and a hand-knit fuchsia-and-purple sweater into her nylon tote.

"Who knows?" the governor had remarked the previous afternoon, a sudden twinkle of amusement lighting his eyes when she'd assured him of her cooperation. "This trip might not be a total loss. If you're lucky, maybe you'll turn up a handsome Greek to help you forget about the past."

The suggestion had struck a nerve. "I certainly hope not," she'd retorted, color staining her cheeks. "Even if I were ready to give the man-woman thing another try at this point, I wouldn't choose a Greek. Not even if he were the last man on earth!"

And I mean that, she vowed some minutes later, slipping into her pajamas and turning out the light. I'll never get caught in the trap my mother made for herself.

Early childhood memories were Zoe's bittersweet companions Sunday afternoon as she sped south down a sparsely traveled stretch of U.S. 19 toward her destination. Fortunately her recollections of her father were mostly happy ones. She'd been almost nine when he'd drowned in a diving accident in the Gulf. She remembered him well—a tall, dark-haired man who was handsome in that rugged Greek way she still grudgingly admired. She could picture him clearly: warm, outgoing and easily moved to laughter, a man with the spontaneous habit of using his hands when he spoke.

She couldn't remember her mother, Janet Hardin Spritos, laughing much in those days, except when her husband, Yannis, returned with the sponge boats to port. *Andras mou*—my man—she had sometimes greeted him in her halting Greek, slipping her arms about his neck in relief.

Yannis's father, Zoe's Greek grandfather, had died before his son, when Zoe was seven. He was just a memory now, the faintest recollection of a dour, square man in shiny, much-pressed trousers and an open-collared shirt who spent most of his time in the cafés along Athens Street, drinking coffee and smoking the *narguileh,* or eastern Mediterranean water pipe, with his friends.

While he'd been thus occupied, his wife, the *Yaya*, had scrubbed and cooked and rolled out paper-thin *phyllo* on the kitchen table. Later, as his widow, she had followed the time-honored Greek custom of dressing exclusively in black, with the sole exception of her apron. A broad but not soft woman of late middle age, she had arranged her iron-gray hair severely in a bun. And she had muttered to herself sometimes in the rich, expressive language that her twenty-nine-year-old granddaughter had now almost ceased to understand.

As far as Zoe knew, the *Yaya* was still alive, keeping house just for herself these days in the tin-roofed frame dwelling on Pericles Street where once they'd all lived together.

Outside Tarpon Springs on the highway, the chain-owned motel where she'd planned to stay, comfortably removed from the jumble of narrow brick streets she remembered, was already full for the night. Unwillingly she was forced to venture down into the older part of town and check in at the Dolphin Inn, across the street from the bayou.

Despite her reluctance, she had to admit it was a picturesque spot. From the balcony outside her room, she could see the wooden pier where each Epiphany Day the Greek Orthodox bishop stood to throw out the good luck cross for an expectant squadron of young divers.

It was said a fortunate year awaited the one who retrieved it.

Epiphany and the clamor it always evoked were less than a month away. At the moment, the port with its strings of Christmas lights and venerable oaks, its moss-draped vistas of the water, was beautifully serene. Maybe you can maintain some perspective, after all, she told herself. Accomplish what you came to do and escape back into your own life. You're not a little girl anymore.

She wasn't scheduled to meet with either the town elders who had approached Jim Haverhill, or Stavros Kalandris and his sons Stavros, Jr. and Konstantin, until morning. A bit cramped from her long drive and too restless simply to sit and watch television, Zoe decided to hike down to the sponge docks and see for herself what all the shouting was about. Anyway, she thought as she set out wearing deck shoes and her jeans and sweater, it'll be easier to get my first look at things before I meet with anyone.

The route she chose, Grand Boulevard, hardly lived up to its name. Paved with uneven bricks that were partly obscured by rough asphalt patchwork, it departed abruptly from the big old houses that lined the bayou near her motel and wound back through the lower middle-class, almost exclusively Greek neighborhood where she'd lived as a child.

Memories came at her in a rush—stirred by the scent of roasting lamb and rich snatches of laughter and conversation that wafted from some of the modest frame dwellings. The miniature perfection of Saint Michael's Chapel with its stained-glass windows and small sign announcing the hours of services in the Romaic alphabet.

At the corner of Pericles Street, she hesitated momentarily, little shivers touching her skin though it wasn't really cold. Then she turned aside, not ready yet to see the *Yaya*'s house with its clean-swept front porch and concrete urns, the row of metal chairs positioned to take the evening air. With a quickened step, she continued down Athens Street, past the cafés where her grandfather had smoked and played at *tavli*, a sort of backgammon, for endless hours.

It was a route she'd often taken as a child, on errands for the *Yaya* to the market to fetch *kallious*, a kind of salted mackerel, or fresh-baked loaves of bread, perhaps some tangerines and bottled grape leaves, honey, feta cheese and tomatoes.

That afternoon as she picked her way over the broken and uneven pavement, it seemed to her that nothing and everything had changed. The houses were much the same as were the small bakeries with their racks of sweet, calorie-laden confections. Even the faint bouzouki music that was played for the tourists still grew louder as she approached the river.

But the round metal tables that had lined the sidewalks in front of most of the cafés were missing now; only a rawboned frame bar patronized solely by men who stared out at female passersby, causing them to avert their eyes, had anything of the old air. She noted a Chinese restaurant and a unisex hair salon, encroachments of another world.

Yet as she reached the docks she saw that nearly everything there seemed untouched by time. Shrimp boats looking like giant insects with their black booms and drying nets still lined the river, along with vessels of every other description. Out-of-town visitors walked at a desultory pace, browsing in the small, old-fashioned shops with their dusty, bare-board floors, fingering outdoor displays of T-shirts, seashell necklaces and bins of sponges.

I don't believe I'm really here, Zoe thought, a little shaken at the unreality of it all. Crossing Dodacanese Boulevard, she stood in a pensive attitude by the quayside, looking out across the blue waters of the Anclote at the Lemnos Shrimp Company wharf. It had been called the Lemnos Sponge Company when she was a child, and it was to that very dock that they'd brought the body of Yannis Spritos after he had drowned.

Tears welled, though she refused to let them spill. I wonder what life would have been like if he had lived, she thought, giving in to a dangerous fantasy. Maybe *Yaya* and the others finally would have accepted us. By now, I might have been married to one of those beautiful and supremely masculine Greek men Jim was talking about. Maybe this afternoon I'd have been rolling out some *phyllo* pastry of my own.

"Want to go fishing, lady?"

The words, spoken in a deep, arresting voice, were only slightly accented, as if the speaker had a native's fluency in English and had acquired his rich and faintly musical diction only by association.

Turning, Zoe found herself looking into dark, honey-colored eyes so beautiful they took her breath away. Sunlit seas were in those eyes, and islands crowned with white temples under a blazing sun, all the warmth, unself-consciousness and deep vitality she had vowed would never lure her into following in her mother's footsteps.

She couldn't seem to keep herself from staring. A swift, covert appraisal confirmed her first impression. The rest of this man who stood smiling at her in narrow-hipped, faded jeans and a string-knit shirt definitely did them justice.

He was tall—taller than her ex-husband by several inches—with the kind of build that only comes from a lucky combination of good genes, hard work and a generous supply of male hormones. In his mid to late thirties, he carried himself with a natural ease that extended to his smile, a disarming flash of white in the tan of his face.

An absolutely gorgeous man, no doubt about it, she thought. Almost a god. At the very least, a classic hero who has sailed Homer's wine-dark sea. I wonder what it would be like to nestle in those strong arms and kindle a flame of desire in those extraordinary eyes.

Then she gave herself a mental shake. He was Greek, after all, and thus off-limits in her self-imposed scheme of things. She had known it immediately, by the thick, springy texture of his hair, the rough-hewn yet classic features, and most tellingly by the gleam of a gold religious medal against the triangle of chest hair exposed by his open collar.

They were standing beside the moorings of a yacht equipped for sport fishing, one with a sign in its cabin window that proclaimed For Charter in both Greek and English. Something subtly proprietary about his attitude suggested that it belonged to him.

So he really is a boat captain, Zoe thought. Yet whatever he did for a living, this was a man who knew himself and what he wanted, she guessed. Somehow she didn't feel it would be a struggle for him to get it. Instead he would draw it effortlessly to himself by the very considerable force of who he was.

"I don't even know how to fish," she protested in belated answer to his question.

His admiring grin broadened. "Oh, but we can take care of that, if you don't have any other objections."

Despite her intention of turning him down, the traitorous dimple beside her mouth flashed with pleasure. "If I did, I'm sure you'd be able to meet them," she said.

"As it happens, I would." His compelling eyes were lively with interest, and he regarded her quizzically for a moment. "You're a tourist, aren't you?" he asked.

"I suppose you could say that."

Zoe knew she was hedging, but she wasn't about to launch into an account of either her background or assignment with this attractive stranger. He was probably only interested in securing a fare for his sport-fishing business.

He didn't seem to sense that she had offered only a partial truth. Instead he nodded as if satisfied. "I didn't think so at first," he said. "But I haven't seen you around here before. I'd have remembered you, I'm certain."

And I'd have remembered you—whether or not I wanted to, she rejoined silently, recalling her conversation with Jim Haverhill two days before.

"Well, what about the fishing trip?" he repeated, confirming her earlier guess that this was just a commercial proposition, after all.

"Maybe some other time," she said, glancing away.

There really wasn't any future in talking to him. The sun was already low in the sky, and soon it would set, flooding the quaint old dock area with pink-and-magenta light. Without a jacket, she would be chilly in the rapidly falling dusk that would follow. It was high time she checked out the object of her walk and then looked around for a bite of supper before turning in for the night.

Yet suddenly she found herself wanting to get this magnificent Greek's reaction to the sponge-exchange controversy. It can't hurt to find out what the average person is thinking, she rationalized. Even if you couldn't call him average on a bet.

"I was hoping to have a look at the old sponge market that's been in the news lately," she remarked in a casual tone, returning her dark-fringed gaze to his. "Do you suppose you could point me in the right direction?"

A muscle quirked alongside his mouth, as if he understood very well that she was giving him a chance to further their acquaintance. Probably he knew the kind of effect he had on women, and took full advantage of it whenever possible.

"Mind telling me your name?" he asked.

She hesitated only fractionally. "It's Zoe."

If he sensed her reluctance to give it or noticed that she had failed to add a surname, he gave no sign. "That's Greek," he replied promptly. "*Zoe mou, sas agapo.*"

She didn't need a translation. Even for her, the meaning of the words was simple enough, "My life, I love you." But she'd have known it, anyway, even if she hadn't once spoken Greek as a child. She'd have remembered it from her college English classes. Her eyes widened a little at this erudite boat captain who thought nothing of tossing off a quote from one of the romantic poets.

"So it is," she admitted. "But you needn't be of Hellenic descent just because you know the poetry of Byron. You haven't answered my question."

"Oh, yes. The sponge market..." Briefly he seemed to weigh her evasiveness and the unspoken invitation, assess her interest in what he must regard as a situation of purely local concern. Yet there was more than just curiosity about an inquisitive tourist in his beautiful eyes.

Then he gave a little shrug, as if he had decided they needn't resolve every ambiguity between them yet. "I'm Alex," he said, forthrightly holding out his hand. "If you like, I can show you the way. We'll discuss my fee later, over drinks aboard the boat."

Two

Her hand resting in his, Zoe felt a tingle of awareness, as if the magnetism of this tall scion of Mediterranean gods were a tangible thing. Fee, she repeated
to herself, a little taken aback. Can he be serious? Yet
she didn't pull away, or quibble about the statement.
Almost absently she noted the calluses on his palm
that spoke of physical labor, the sense of warmth and
quiet strength his touch imparted.

There's a part of me who would follow him anywhere, she realized in surprise, even though he's a
Greek and a perfect stranger. Thank heaven I'm too
levelheaded to let my most renegade nature have its
way.

He seemed to take her silence for assent. "Come on,
then," he said, dropping her hand and guiding her effortlessly with a light touch at the small of her back.
"The sponge exchange isn't very exciting these days,

I'm afraid. But I can tell you a little of its history. It used to be squarely at the heart of this community."

She didn't reply, and they walked the half block or so to the old landmark in silence. Peering through the iron fence at the large weed-and-sandspur-choked courtyard surrounded by tan stucco stalls, Zoe honestly couldn't see what the fuss was all about. The empty building, with its tin-roofed arcade and central water tower, looked as if it had been shuttered and neglected for years.

When she'd been a child and living in this town, perhaps half of the grilled wooden doors to the stalls had still been open commercially on market days. Sponges threaded in ring-shaped bunches had been piled outside them, waiting to be disposed of by the auctioneer.

The newspaper accounts she'd read had correctly stated that the structure was in bad repair. The tin awning visibly sagged, and some of the stucco had crumbled to reveal the underlying buff brick structure. Much of the paint and varnish on the wooden trim had weathered away.

Automatically she jiggled the gate. It was locked. "Darn," she said, moving off from him a little along the iron fence.

"Maybe it's only jammed." His back to her, Alex fiddled with the lock. A moment later the gate stood open. "After you," he said. "I warn you, there's not much to see."

Stepping ahead of him into the courtyard, she gave him a surreptitious glance. I know that gate was securely locked, she thought. It's almost as if he has professional lock-picking talents. Or a key.

Then she set speculation aside as he began to tell her about the history of the place and how sponge fishing had gotten started in Tarpon Springs just before the turn of the century.

"In 1891, an American, John Cheyney, and a Greek, John Cocoris, started the sponge-fishing industry here," he explained. "They employed some local fishermen to start, but the hauls were too rich, and there were too few workers available with the skill, daring and capacity for hard work the job required. By 1905, Cocoris was importing divers from the Greek islands of Kalimnos and Simi and Kalki, in the Aegean off the coast of Turkey, near Rhodes.

"You see, the art of sponge diving had been perfected in that area long before classical times. Originally the Phoenicians discovered it, and later it even evolved into a competition at the ancient Olympic games. Plato mentioned it in his work, and soldiers in the Persian Wars used sponges from the isles of the Southern Dodacanese to pad their armor...."

As he spoke, Alex gestured in a way that made Zoe think of her father. It was as if the movements were an integral part of his discourse.

Then he fell silent, giving her a self-deprecatory smile. He was standing very close. "Probably I'm telling you more about all this than you care to know," he said.

Intensely conscious of his physical presence, Zoe had to admit she'd been fascinated with the chronological perspective he was providing. She told him so, adding, "There must have been a thriving industry here at one time, if the size of this place is any indication. What happened? Did most of the sponges out of these waters die?"

Her companion shook his head. "Sponges are animals, and they reproduce like other living things... replenish themselves unless they're taken indiscriminantly. Harvesting them on a grand scale just isn't profitable any more. But you're right...in the old days, they say, there were maybe two hundred boats operating out of this little port. Huge auctions were held here in the exchange.

"Now nobody wants to work out on the water in the heat of summer or the cold of winter for maybe thirty or forty days at a time, seeing nothing but the Gulf and the other divers. For a younger, better-educated generation, there are easier and more lucrative ways to earn a living."

How lucrative can the charter-boat business be, Zoe wondered, remembering the snatch of poetry he'd recited. But she had to admit he'd chosen a romantic way to channel his obvious initiative and intelligence. He probably had an inborn love of the sea that he couldn't quell.

"I can understand how the old men feel about this place, though," he added, as if he'd given the matter a good deal of consideration. "It represents a time gone by, when they were young and virile, with red blood and hot desire in their veins. They're sad to see a way of life disappearing in which they've sunk their best manhood years."

Zoe regarded him thoughtfully. She couldn't help liking the way he'd stated his affection for the old people of his town in the same breath with an unconscious affirmation of masculine pride.

Too bad he's probably a chauvinist like all the rest of them, she thought, and unable to see that women can have the same need for accomplishment and a

place in the world. Even her beloved father had been
blind to that reality, insisting that her mother stay at
home with the *Yaya*, who hated her, and keep the
home fires burning against his return.

"What do *you* think about this place?' she asked,
posing her original question. "Should it be turned into
a shopping plaza? Or kept as a monument?"

He was a long time in answering. "I agree that it
should be developed," he said finally. "Times change.
The improved economic base will be good for everyone...help create jobs for the grandsons and the
granddaughters of the old divers."

Zoe hoped he didn't catch the light flush that spread
over her cheeks. Here she'd been silently accusing him
of male prejudice and he'd quite casually put the
matter to rest. "But it's too bad, isn't it," she said
quickly, "to see tradition go by the wayside? I mean,
slick shops and planters filled with flowers won't
prompt children to find out about their heritage...or
outsiders like me to ask questions."

For a moment his honey-colored eyes glinted with
the curiosity they'd held earlier, as if he found her interest a bit beyond the norm. Then he nodded. "I
worry about that, too," he agreed.

"And?"

"Those who want to keep this place as it is and
those who are determined to change it are each set on
having their way. Unfortunately neither side seems
very willing to compromise."

Would that the men I have to meet with in the
morning be as reasonable, Zoe said to herself. In a few
short minutes she had gone beyond the admiration of
this tall Greek's physical attributes and obvious char-
isma to begin liking him as a person—a thoughtful,

considerate man who cared about history, progress and people, in the bargain.

He makes me sorry I have the background I do, she thought. If I weren't so mistrustful of my Greek inheritance, I might want to explore a real relationship with him. Unfortunately I'm too old-fashioned to partake of whatever fleeting intimacy we might share.

"Well..." she said, looking up at him regretfully. "Thank you, Alex. I appreciated the tour. *And* the history lesson...more than I can say."

"It was my pleasure."

With a little sigh, she turned as if to depart. Unexpectedly one capable hand lightly settled on her arm, detaining her. They were still standing very close, and for one wild moment she thought that he might kiss her. But all he did was usher her toward the gate.

"Time for the payment of my fee," he said firmly, shutting it behind them and striking out in the direction of the boat. "Over drinks, as we agreed."

Zoe went weak in the knees at the thought of what he might be proposing. "I...didn't agree to anything," she objected a little breathlessly. "And I certainly didn't think you were serious...about a fee..."

One dark brow lifted a little. "Of course I was serious," he said. "Your agreement was a tacit one. It's not ladylike to renege now that my services have been rendered."

Effectively silenced, Zoe allowed him to escort her to the dockside where he'd originally spoken to her. But she had absolutely no intention of letting him have his way.

"Here," he said matter-of-factly, pulling on the charter yacht's mooring lines. "Take my hand and step aboard while I hold the rope."

Firmly she planted her feet on the sidewalk. "I'll do no such thing," she replied.

"Ah, Zoe." To her surprise he seemed to be laughing at her, though there was no mistaking the gleam of sensual interest in his eyes. "I promise I won't ravish you unless you ask me to."

She flushed again, her cheeks staining crimson this time so that they reflected the evening color that was beginning to tint the sky.

"How am I supposed to know that?" she countered even while some perverse spirit made her do as he was suggesting.

A moment later he was beside her, allowing the line to slacken again so that they drifted out a little from the seawall. "You're supposed to rely on your feminine instinct," he said.

She didn't answer and his mouth curved a little at the corners. "I like to watch the sunset from the water," he added, tactfully changing the subject. "Even anchored here in the river. The silhouettes of the shrimp boats and old buildings make an attractive contrast, don't you think?"

Still she didn't respond, but simply stood there, ready to refuse any effort on his part to get her inside the cabin.

"I assure you I don't plan to watch it from inside, tangled up in one of the bunks with you...pleasant as that might be," he added, unerringly targeting her thoughts. "Sit down and make yourself comfortable while I get our drinks."

Feeling like a fool, she took one of the swivel fighting chairs that faced the stern-mounted rod pockets. You're a few feet from the street and there are people passing by, she reminded herself. And he's not one of the old gods, even though he looks the part. Heaven knows there's little enough adventure in your life.

By the time Alex had returned with an exotic-looking bottle and two little gold-rimmed glasses, she'd recovered her composure. "Ouzo," he said, pouring for both of them. "It might be a bit much if you haven't tried it before. Let me know if you'd prefer something lighter."

Determined now not to seem sheltered or a prude, Zoe sipped at the fiery liquid without complaint. A little of this could go quite powerfully to my head, she realized. I'd better take care to stay sober if I'm going to spend much time in his company.

Yet as he took the chair beside hers and stretched out his long legs so that his feet were propped on the rail, he seemed deceptively manageable and at ease.

"Talking about history and tradition reminds me of a fantasy I've always had about this place," he said. "Here in America, Tarpon Springs is considered quaint, even historical. Yet compared with the old country, it's as new as tomorrow. It doesn't even have a myth associated with it.

"If this were Greece, Anclote would have been a nymph before she was a river. One of the gods—Poseidon, probably—would have swooped down to violate her. Afterward, Aphrodite, his jealous lover, would have pursued poor Anclote with threats of vengeance.

"The nymph's patron—Artemis, perhaps, because she had been a virgin—would have intervened to save her, changing her into a stream and rescuing her unborn child. Of course, the baby would have grown up to be a hero, part man and part god, creator of the

sponge and fishing industry that sprang up along Anclote's banks.''

Throughout his fanciful supposition Zoe had remained silent, vividly aware of the sexual nature of his
allegory. "I didn't know that Aphrodite and Poseidon had an affair of the heart," she said at last.

"Ah, but they did. He fell in love with her and intervened on her behalf when her jealous husband,
Hephaestus, trapped her with her previous lover, Ares,
under a bronze net of his own design."

It was all a bit too lecherous for Zoe's taste, but . . .
"I rather like your tale about Anclote," she admitted. "Even if she didn't have much to say about her
fate. Tell me something, Alex . . . were you born in
Greece? You seem to have such a feeling for the
place."

Stretching, he laced his fingers together behind his
head as he looked up at the clouds, which were slowly
transforming themselves from rose to magenta to the
deepest shades of indigo. "You're right, I do care for
it, and all the richness it has bequeathed me," he said.
"But, no, I'm second generation American. I traveled to Greece and to the islands I told you about when
I was in my late twenties. Someday, when the time is
right, I hope to go again."

They fell into a companionable silence as night
drained the last color from the sky. Overhead Zoe
noted the first pinpricks of stars. When Alex refilled
her glass she accepted it with a brief thanks and sipped
at the contents, willfully ignoring any danger. It's as
if even the forces of nature are conspiring to make me
forget my prejudices, she thought. The hush that had
settled over the river as they sat side by side seemed to
creep past her defenses with the stealth of the ouzo and

her own instinctive regard for him, calming her and making her relax for the first time since she'd returned to the town where she was born.

Accordingly, she was unprepared, almost defenseless, when he brought up the matter of payment again.

"I propose to be reimbursed for my services by your truthful answer to a single question," he said suddenly, taking his feet down from the rail and turning to her, his eyes gleaming at her in the dark.

"I...can't imagine what you'd want to know about me," she blurted, setting her drink on the deck at her feet.

"Nothing that extraordinary. Do you agree to my terms?"

On the brink of trusting him, she wavered. What if he asks whether or not I'm attracted to him, she thought. Would I dare answer truthfully to that—even to myself?

"All right," she agreed finally. "Provided it's a question I'm willing to answer, I'll be honest with you."

"Fair enough." Unobtrusively, he took possession of her hand. "Back when we met I couldn't help wondering something," he went on. "Though I didn't quite ask you then...I got the feeling it was something you didn't want me to know."

Her large brown eyes meeting his, Zoe waited, certain now she'd guessed what his question would be.

"Something about you made me wonder if you were Greek," he went on, not disappointing her. "And your name just confirmed that feeling. But if so, why would you want to keep that a secret?"

Though she'd prepared herself for this type of question, expecting someone to ask it, she couldn't seem to help the stricken look that came over her face.

"Don't tell me if you'd rather not," he said gently after a moment. "Your debt is forgiven, anyway."

Zoe shook her head though she wouldn't quite return his gaze. "No," she said. "It's all right. In answer to your question, I *am* Greek and I'm not. At least, I don't want to be. You're right ... I didn't want to tell you."

For the first time since they'd met, Alex seemed at a loss. "I'm afraid I don't understand," he admitted finally with a little frown.

"That's not surprising." Thankful for the cloak of approaching darkness, she continued to look out at the bulking shapes of the shrimp trawlers as they floated on the water. "My father was Greek and my mother an orphan of English and Irish descent from Kentucky," she confessed in a low voice. "His relatives never accepted her. After he died...they as much as sent her packing. She wasn't too well, and we had a terrible time making ends meet until I got through school, though she insisted I get an education. When I finally had a job and was able to help with expenses, she died. I've ... never forgiven them."

Swearing softly, Alex took her face in his hands. For all their obvious strength, they were extremely gentle.

"That's a terrible story," he said. "On behalf of all Greeks, I humbly beg your pardon. Some of our old people are unbearably clannish, I know, though things are changing. With the kind of memories you have, I'm amazed you would talk to me at all."

For Zoe, his kindness was harder to bear than if he'd given her an argument. To her acute distress, her eyes filled with tears.

"Ah, Zoe. Don't..." With one bluntly manicured finger, he brushed a teardrop from her cheek.

But it was like trying to stem the tide. Old hurts were welling inexorably to the surface, and she sat there softly weeping, her wet lashes like the points of stars.

It was inevitable that he would put his arms around her. With a little sigh, he drew her up against him to stroke her hair. The scent of him—clean hair and sun-warmed skin, an indefinable masculine aroma unadulterated by cologne—filled her nostrils. She had an overwhelming sensation of comfort and refuge.

Finally he drew back a little, looked at her and wiped away a trace of mascara. "Better?" he asked in that deep, almost musical voice. "Sometimes it helps to cry."

"A little better," she said.

Neither of them said anything more for a moment. One hand resting lightly on her arm, he tilted her chin upward a little so that he could search her eyes. A moment ago, she realized, they'd still been strangers. Now, because of his comforting gesture, there was an added dimension between them. In it her strong attraction to him arose again.

"I...guess I was being silly," she said, casting about for something to say. "In most ways, I guess, I'm a liberated woman. But whenever I feel like crying, I don't seem to be able to stop the tears."

"Greek men have always been liberated," he answered. "They cry...or dance or make love... according to what they feel."

Somehow, without her meaning it to happen, her arms slipped about his neck, even as he lowered his mouth to hers. His kiss—so blunt and tender—was tentative at first, as if he didn't want to frighten her away.

For her part, Zoe was overwhelmed. All the compassion she'd sensed in him, all the sweet solace she knew he could provide, were communicated to her in that moment, in a language that spanned cultural biases and needed no translation.

It was a message made all the more welcome by ouzo and the tug of bitter memories—even if its sexual overtones couldn't be denied. Though she had dated a few times before and after her marriage, Blaine Walker had been her only lover. During the brief years of their marriage, his kisses had inevitably been the overture to a selfish passion. He'd granted her release only as an afterthought, leaving her perennially hunger stricken and lonely.

Just the taste of this man promised more—a warmth that would flood every part of her body, passion spiraling out of control. She sensed an innate generosity that would ensure satisfaction so deep it must permeate the very center of her being.

Not pausing to consider that he was still essentially a stranger, she parted her lips beneath his in a mute little gesture of surrender.

If she'd guessed before at his power, she needed no further evidence. Drawing her to her feet, he molded her to his hard male length. Firm and muscular in the faded jeans, his thighs pressed against hers. Beneath the bulky sweater, her breasts were crushed against his chest.

"Zoe, Zoe..." he said, one hand tangling in the short blond curls at her nape while the other dropped from the small of her back to tilt her lower body up against him. "Do you know how very good you are to hold?"

Then he was kissing her again, covering her mouth with his so forcefully that she couldn't reply. Strenuous and bold, his tongue entered to explore the moist access she had offered, make it thoroughly his. She felt something in her begin to give way, a certain separateness. Incredibly, her most reckless self was ready to jettison all her hard-won defenses, blindly and impetuously to follow where he led.

As if he sensed the depth of her capitulation and knew that she would regret it, Alex drew back a little.

"*Zoe mou,*" he said, his face in shadow. "Forgive me. I didn't mean to overpower you in that way."

Still held lightly in his arms, she felt her pulse racing. "Don't apologize," she whispered. "It was *my* fault as much as yours. I...encouraged you."

"Honesty, as agreed." His eyes were full of approval as he leaned down to brush her mouth with just the trace of a kiss. "And such a giving nature. I don't want to drive you away by taking advantage of that."

Confounded by his old-fashioned gallantry, Zoe couldn't think of a reply.

"You're staying for a while, aren't you?" he asked after a small silence had lengthened between them. "Not leaving in the morning, so that I'll always regret my forbearance?"

"I imagine I'll be here for several days."

"Good." He smiled, his teeth white and healthy-looking against his face. "Then we'll have a chance to see each other again. I want you to have a good opinion of me.''

Again she didn't speak, and he ruffled the fingers of one hand through her hair. "Naturally curly, isn't it?" he remarked. "The Greek coming out in you, despite your best intentions. Would you like to walk down the block and get a sandwich?''

The suggestion brought a smile to her face. Without realizing it, she had become very hungry, indeed, ready to eat almost anything, even if it had to be *gyros* and Greek salad with hunks of feta cheese and brown, piquant olives.

"I'd like that very much," she said.

Allowing Alex to help her ashore, she accompanied him to a tiny waterfront café where they partook of precisely the meal she had imagined. Yet somehow, though they talked of many things, he never discussed his sport-fishing business, nor did she describe her position on the governor's staff.

"Well, Zoe..." he said when finally he'd paid the bill and they were back out on the sidewalk again. "Perhaps I'd better walk you to your car."

For a moment she was disoriented. "I...didn't bring it," she stammered, suddenly aware of the tangle of dark streets that separated her from her motel.

"Where are you staying, then? With relatives? No...I suppose not, considering the way you feel...."

Ignoring his reference to her family and shaking her head at her own improvidence, she gave him the name of her motel.

"I'll drive you," he offered, leading her to a charcoal-gray Mercedes sedan with smoked-glass windows that had been parked across from the yacht all evening. Charter-boat captain or not, she thought, apparently he makes quite a handsome living.

At the Dolphin Inn, Alex insisted on accompanying her upstairs to her second-floor room and making certain her key would fit the lock. She pushed the door part way open and turned to him.

"Well, I guess this is good-night," she said, all too aware of what had passed between them and wondering if he would try to come in.

He didn't. "When am I going to see you again?" he asked instead, lifting her chin with one finger in the way he had before.

"I...I don't know," she responded, adding to herself that it would be a disaster to get mixed up with him—even if he was the most beautiful man she'd ever met, and probably one of the nicest in the bargain.

His mouth curved, as if he could read her thoughts. "Have breakfast with me tomorrow," he proposed, naming a small Greek pastry shop and coffeehouse and suggesting they meet at nine.

Her appointment with Stavros Kalandris was for eleven. "I'm not sure I should," she began. "Actually I'm here on business. I really don't have much time...."

Alex shook his head. She could see that he was laughing at her gently. "To hell with business," he said. "For once let your spontaneous Greek self do the deciding. That way, you won't object when I kiss you good-night."

Three

———

Memories of holding Alex's tall body in her arms and the tender imprint of his mouth were like nectar to Zoe as she snuggled down beneath the covers of her king-size bed.

With only slight encouragement, he'd managed easily what others had only tried to do: breach the thorny defenses she'd erected after her divorce from Blaine.

As unexpected as that was, she found it nothing short of astonishing that the man who'd accomplished it was Greek, someone she'd have sworn was doomed to failure from the start.

Maybe I was right, she thought, hugging her pillow as she conjured up the warmth and amusement in his eyes, his broad, sweet shoulders. Maybe he's no mortal at all, but one of the old gods—Poseidon, because of his occupation—stepping out of the myth he made.

She amended her fantasy as she drifted into sleep. The handsome boat captain who threatened to destroy her most closely held prejudices as he reawakened her heart was not Poseidon, but Apollo. Her inner self whispered that truth as it gained the upper hand in dreams. His thoughtful intelligence and that passionate yet temperate nature had given him away. Even disguised in jeans and a string-knit shirt, he was none other than the patron of Delphi and heaven's charioteer, she was certain, someone with whom any impressionable young nymph would fall madly in love.

Cold reason returned as daylight seeped into her room around the edges of the heavy motel curtains. Reluctantly opening her eyes, Zoe surveyed her unfamiliar surroundings. Without benefit of ouzo or Alex's presence to justify it, her behavior of the night before seemed foolish, if not downright embarrassing—particularly in view of her heated reply to Jim Haverhill only a few days earlier.

Like Yannis Spritos, Alex of the honey-dark eyes would belong to a large family. He would have a stern and silent father, a disapproving mother and more than a few relatives who would cut dead any girl raised in the American mode, even though she was half a Hellene by birth.

If she let her emotions lure her into a serious alliance with him, she'd find herself trapped by the same xenophobic, male-dominated culture that had stamped out her mother's spirit.

It's best not to tempt fate, she decided as she considered his invitation to breakfast at the little Greek pastry shop across from Saint Nicholas Cathedral. I just won't go.

A quick glance at her watch on the bedside table showed a quarter after eight already. In forty-five minutes, he would be waiting for her—glancing at his own watch with mounting impatience and deciding to seek her out at her motel. To sidestep a confrontation, she would have to be quick on her feet.

Throwing back the covers, she scrambled into the shower and faced the heavy spray as a kind of penance. Minutes later she was vigorously towel-drying her short, bronze-gold curls and struggling to fit her still faintly damp body into underwear and hose. She made a face at herself in the mirror as she donned a gray wool gabardine suit designed to give her an air of authority at that day's meetings. All right, she thought, I know I'm behaving like a coward. But that's better than acting like a fool.

Dressed and ready, she felt determined not to show her face near the sponge docks for fear of running into him. Instead she decided to kill an hour or so at Howard Park, on the Gulf. Its man-made beach hadn't existed when she'd lived in Tarpon Springs as a child, so it wouldn't stir any memories.

She realized the tactical error she'd made as she crossed the causeway and parked beneath rustling sabal palms. Imprisoned behind the wheel of her car by business clothes, she had far too much time to think about Alex and lost opportunity as she watched more suitably attired beachcombers strolling along the sand.

She was feeling more than a little regret some time later as she arrived at the offices of Kalandris Enterprises. But her choice had been made, and she tried to push Alex from her mind. Absently she noted how the firm's modern reception area, with its complete lack of the usual ethnic decoration, didn't even hint at its owners' Greek heritage.

But there could be no mistaking Stavros Kalandris's nationality as his secretary ushered Zoe into his presence. An energetic-looking man in his early sixties, he had the craggy, weathered face of a Homeric warrior. Deep lines were etched on either side of a firm yet generous mouth. Shaggy, emphatic brows heightened her impression of strength.

She had the haunting feeling that somehow she should know him. Even the deep yet faintly musical timbre of his voice as he greeted her gave her pause. With relief she saw that his eyes, though lively with humor and admiration, were brown, not the tawny, translucent color that came so readily to mind.

He probably knew my father, she thought, voicing gratitude that he could arrange to see her on such short notice.

"But of course, Miss Walker. *Parakalo*." He gave her a brilliant smile. "It's always a pleasure...to do business with a beautiful woman."

What an attractive man he is even if he doesn't mean a word of it, she decided. Wily as old Zeus himself, and both charming and physically powerful. Thank heaven he's the right age to be my father. Otherwise I'd begin to think this trip is a conspiracy to challenge my opinion of Greek men.

Imprisoning her hand a moment longer than necessary, as if he wished to take her mettle, Stavros Kalandris turned toward a handsome, somber-faced young man who stood beside his desk.

"Miss Walker, my son Konstantin," he said. "Kon's our family accountant—or numbers jockey, as I believe it's called these days."

Zoe shook the unsmiling Konstantin's hand. "My pleasure," she said, glancing back at his father. "Jim Haverhill sends his best. He asked me to express his appreciation of your willingness to discuss the sponge-exchange issue."

Stavros nodded. "We hope to resolve any worries he might have concerning our project."

He's not giving an inch, thought Zoe, maintaining a pleasant look. "That's our hope, too," she said, taking the seat he offered. "Would you like to begin by bringing me up to date on your plans? Or would you prefer to delay a few minutes? I understand that another of your sons, Stavros, Jr., will also be joining us."

For a moment, Stavros, Sr. gave her a blank look. "Oh, of course," he said, a strong note of pride and affection warming his voice as he glanced just past her shoulder. "You mean Alex. Here he is now, Miss Walker. May I introduce my eldest son, Stavros Alexander, Jr., our family attorney and the manager of our boat-building concern."

Scraping her chair awkwardly on the thick carpet, Zoe leapt to her feet. This can't be happening, she thought. But though she almost pinched herself in disbelief, *her* Alex of the night before was standing here in an exquisitely tailored business suit, a quizzical if faintly ironic expression on his face.

Hot color rose to her cheeks. She felt cornered, caught, humiliated—and something else she didn't want to nail down with words. He must be furious with me for standing him up like that, she thought.

Probably he'll see to it that I don't get anywhere with his father.

"I . . . I'm sorry about this morning," she faltered when he didn't speak. "Forgive me. I thought it would be for the best. . . ."

But he didn't seem about to denounce her. "It doesn't matter," he said, appraising her as he held out his hand. "The Fates have spun their web, Zoe Walker. And so we can't help meeting again, as they ordained."

Feeling abysmally foolish didn't seem to blunt her strong sense of vulnerability as she let her hand rest in his. Once again he was standing too close, and she caught a remembered whiff of his provocative and totally masculine scent. Stop it, she warned herself. You can't even let an affair with him cross your mind.

"I should have left you a note, or something," she acknowleged, trying to regain her equilibrium. "I wasn't sure how to call. . . ."

The excuse sounded lame even in her own ears. Doubtless he recognized it for what it was: her first line of defense against the headlong rush of feeling he seemed so naturally able to evoke. Too late she realized that it also raised quite a few unanswered questions. Her flush deepened at the spark of interest in his father's eyes and the unabashed curiosity that lighted Konstantin's face.

"So," said Stavros, regarding the two of them. "I see no introductions are needed."

Unable to frame an answer, Zoe looked at Alex beseechingly.

"We met last night, by Uncle Tryfon's boat," he supplied. "Afterward we had dinner together. I suppose it was something of a coincidence. But it would have been difficult, wouldn't it have, Father, for Miss Walker to avoid either the Kalandrises or their property in this town?''

Afterward? Zoe repeated the word to herself in dismay. He makes it sound as if he lured me into his bunk, after all, she thought.

But his father didn't appear to draw any unfounded conclusions. "That's true," he said with a chuckle, obviously pleased that Alex had chosen to impress her with the extent of their family holdings. She imagined she caught a hint of fond approval, too, that his tall namesake had already succeeded in making her acquaintance.

I suppose it's obvious to the most incurious onlooker that I'm attracted to him, she thought ruefully as she retook her seat. Well, let them speculate all they want. Before I'm finished, both Alex Kalandris and his father will be convinced that this is strictly a business matter with me.

It wasn't easy to avoid meeting Alex's eyes as he went to lounge against a low filing cabinet directly facing her. She could feel his gaze on her skin like a touch as his father spoke of razing that portion of the sponge exchange that was structurally unsound and converting the remainder of the old building into specialty shops and restaurants.

The development would not only make money for him and his tenants but also improve the economic base of the town, Stavros said. "Gus Andriotis and his friends could have bought that property for pennies not very long ago," he added, naming the potential rival for Blaine in the upcoming congressional primary who had approached Jim Haverhill about purchasing the old landmark. "But it was a neglected eyesore, and they didn't have any interest then. They expected the owner, whoever that might be, to go on paying the taxes and keep it around for the old people, in case they wanted to notice it was there.

"As soon as we buy it and try to make something worthwhile of it—" he snapped his fingers "—they say we are violating tradition. *I* say what we're doing is good. It will create jobs and bring more tourists . . . be good for the town."

It was Alex's argument of the night before, one he said he'd arrived at after much consideration. He'd also expressed sympathy for the opposite point of view. Involuntarily she glanced at him. But he was enough of a businessman not to let any private scruples show in his face.

Whatever her own opinion, Zoe had to argue Andriotis's and the governor's case. "I can't believe it would be good for business in such a small, closely knit community to go against the wishes of so many people," she remarked quietly, looking back at his father again. "We're aware you have an interest in the property that exceeds your purchase price. Why not recoup it from the state and remain friends with everyone?"

Stavros glanced at his other son. "Kon?"

"Naturally any price we might place on the property . . . if we consented to sell it . . . would have to reflect the opportunity cost of foregoing development." The family accountant named a figure Zoe considered extravagant. "Is the state prepared to meet that demand?"

She didn't express her skepticism aloud. "That would be up to the legislature to answer, of course," she replied. "If you'll agree to wait until it reconvenes in special session next month, a bill will be introduced to approve purchase at fair market value.''

"And if we and the state can't agree on what the value is?" It was Stavros speaking again.

Zoe shrugged. There was always condemnation, though she didn't plan to mention that.

Alex leaned forward a little. "Every day that we wait construction costs go up," he interposed. "If it ever came to a court battle and the state lost its case, we could recover those costs in damages."

"I'm aware of that." Zoe's eyes rested briefly, unwillingly, on the shape of his mouth. "We're hoping for a voluntary delay...and a negotiated settlement...in the interest of preserving the community's heritage."

There was a small silence in the room. Zoe folded her hands in her lap. Cooperate or not, she told them silently. My main objective is to get out of town before my grandmother finds out I'm around.

She was almost certain that the answer would be *no*. Stavros's monologue about Gus Andriotis and his friends had held out little hope. Thus she was surprised when he requested time to consider whether they should discuss the matter further. "You're meeting with Gus this afternoon, I understand," he said. "Decide for yourself if this is an election issue with him or if it really matters. We can talk again tomorrow."

"What about this evening?" Quietly Alex put the question. "Perhaps Miss Walker would care to have dinner with us...." He paused. "Or rather cocktails, as I have a dinner engagement."

To Zoe's chagrin, he appeared to catch her flash of interest in his evening plans. Then he glanced back at his father again, and a look of understanding passed between them. "I'm sure your mother would be delighted to meet her," Stavros said. "Can you make it, Miss Walker? About six o'clock."

Outside in the company's gravel parking lot, Alex caught up with her. "I won't ask you about this morning," he said, lightly taking her arm. "I trust we can expect you to be faithful about keeping this evening's appointment?"

To her great irritation, Zoe found herself blushing again. Why can't I control my emotions when I'm around this man, she wondered. "I'll be there," she retorted, not pausing to choose her words with care. "I hope you won't be forced to keep your dinner date waiting."

Alex narrowed his magnificent eyes in the brilliant sunlight. "I don't see how that would be possible," he replied with just a touch of the traditional Greek male arrogance she so deplored, "since I'm having dinner with you."

Her meeting later with Gus Andriotis and his cohorts was a moderate success. Pleased that the state proposed to intervene on their behalf, they declared themselves willing to await the outcome of Jim Haverill's proposed legislation. As she walked out of Andriotis's storefront office on Tarpon Avenue that afternoon, Alex was still very much on her mind. She didn't see the chunky, elderly woman with her threadbare black dress and shawl until it was too late. There was a little jolt as they bumped into each other, the force of their contact knocking a package from the woman's arms.

For a moment, Zoe simply stared, adrenaline coursing through her veins even while she was held fast by a chilling paralysis. "*Yaya*?" she croaked, the single word catching in her throat.

But the kindly old face that peered into hers wasn't familiar, after all. "I know you . . . yes?" the woman asked in her broken English, her parcel forgotten.

"No. No . . . I was mistaken. *Me synhorite, kyria.* I'm sorry for making you drop your things." Hastily Zoe bent to retrieve the bundle of clean men's shirts, which the grandmother probably had just picked up at the cleaners for a pampered son or grandson.

The woman smiled at Zoe's attempt to speak her language. "*Sas parakalo*," she said. "Is all right." Still smiling, she shuffled off down the sidewalk in her worn carpet slippers.

If Zoe had needed something to convince her it would be foolhardy to remain in Tarpon Springs and get involved with Alex, her moment of sheer panic at meeting the anonymous Greek woman who resembled her own grandmother had provided it. Firmly resolving to rebuff any overtures from him, she parked her car in the circle drive before the Kalandrises' bayou-front mansion early that evening.

The house itself was about what she'd expected. A two-story tile-roofed, Mediterranean-style structure, it lacked the Ionic columns and Greek-key architectural trim that adorned several neighboring homes. But though it was quite handsome and obviously reflected the family's wealth, she couldn't picture Alex living there.

A young woman about Zoe's age, very pregnant and with a strong family resemblance to Alex, met her at the door. "How do you do, Miss Walker?" she said, smiling pleasantly. "Please come in. I'm Theo, sister of Kon and Alex, whom you met this afternoon. The rest of the family is waiting for you in the living room."

To Zoe's discomfort, it appeared that the entire Kalandris clan, or most of it, had assembled in the ornate, old-fashioned room to hear the family patriarch turn down her proposal. With modest grace, Theo introduced each of her relatives in turn—her mother, the stylish and still-beautiful Cristina Kalandris, Kon's wife, Stefania, her own husband, Nick Nikolaides. "Uncle Tryfon and my brother Adonis are out with the boat," she added. "They should be returning at any moment."

Softly Zoe acknowledged each person's greeting. Before she could get down to the purpose of her visit, she knew, there were pleasantries to be observed. She tried not to let her heart skip a beat when Alex asked in his deep voice what she would like to drink.

He had the grace not to suggest ouzo again. "Perrier and lime, if that's all right," she replied, primly taking a seat beside Stavros's wife. She was uncomfortably aware that her severely cut suit made her seem staid and proper, indeed, when compared with Cristina's banana-yellow silk and Stefania's smashing red pants outfit.

No mousy colors for *these* Greek women, she thought in amazement. I wonder if their clothing reflects a modicum of self-determination.

Then she forced herself to listen to what Alex was saying. "You mentioned Uncle Tryfon's boat, Theo," he remarked as he handed Zoe her drink. "Last night,

Miss Walker thought it was mine. She took me for a charter-boat captain.''

Theo smiled. ''A natural mistake.''

''Which your brother didn't take the trouble to correct.''

Her reply sounded peevish, as she was all too aware. But she could have throttled him for airing even the most innocuous details of their meeting in front of his family. What must they think of her for taking up with a stranger—even if he was one of them?

Sensing her chagrin, perhaps, Stavros reached over to pat her hand. ''You weren't so far off the mark, my dear young lady,'' he said. ''As I told you, Alex is our boat builder...the president and general manager of Kalandris Yachts, a position he inherited from his grandfather.''

''That's a surprising occupation for an attorney,'' she said.

Alex shrugged, an unmistakable glint still visible in his eyes. ''Not really. We make large...and very expensive...sailing yachts. They have beauty and almost a living spirit...the kind of romance, if you will, that you can't find in a court of law.''

She didn't reply, and Stavros changed the subject. ''Alex tells me you're half Greek, Miss Walker,'' he began, asking the dreaded question she had been lulled into thinking she could escape. ''I should have recognized it. Do you have relatives here in Tarpon Springs?''

Somehow she made her voice come out almost normally. ''Not many these days, I'm afraid. My father, Yannis Spritos, was killed in a boating accident when I was a child. We moved away from here after that.''

" 'Spritos...' " he repeated. "Can it be possible? You're not the granddaughter of old Kalliopaea, who lives over on Pericles Street?"

"The same." To Zoe, the admission seemed to die in her throat. Please, she begged him silently. Don't ask if I've been to see her yet.

Thankfully he did not, probably because it didn't occur to him that she would neglect to visit her own grandmother. "But that makes us relatives!" he exclaimed. "By marriage, anyway. Did you realize that young Nick here, Theo's husband, is your cousin... the grandson of Fotis Nikolaides, Kalliopaea's brother?"

Certain that her face must be the color of chalk under her light tan, Zoe tried to summon as much enthusiasm as she could. "But that's wonderful," she said.

Family talk took up the next twenty minutes or so. Theo, it turned out, had been in Zoe's class in school, while Stefania had been several years ahead of them. Sick inside, Zoe bore it as best she could, praying they wouldn't ask any too-personal questions.

Finally Alex rescued her. "If you don't mind, father," he said, "I'm sure Miss Walker would like to hear your decision on the governor's proposal. As I mentioned earlier, I have a dinner engagement, and I understand she has one, too."

Not with you, Zoe told him silently even while she telegraphed her gratitude.

From the moment he had declared her "family," Stavros had dropped his business manner altogether. "Of course," he said. "Your grandmother must be expecting you. I wish we could persuade both of you to remain. My mother has made her famous *dolmathes* this afternoon.''

Graciously Cristina Kalandris echoed her husband's regret.

''The *dolmathes* sound wonderful,'' Zoe said, trying to ignore Alex's obvious assumption that she had accepted his high-handed invitation. ''Thank you anyway for inviting me.''

Stavros beamed. ''Perhaps another time, then. As the governor's able and charming assistant, my dear young lady, you're waiting to hear my answer. It's yes. Earlier, I had almost decided to turn you down. But it's the least we can do, to cooperate with a relative, someone who's almost a member of the family. I'll give the legislature until the end of the special session to make satisfactory arrangements.''

The sudden, heady victory caught Zoe unawares. Somehow—inadequately, she was certain—she thanked him again. ''I promise I'll keep you posted on our progress,'' she said.

Everyone glanced up then as a thin and refined-looking elderly woman appeared in the doorway. Smiling and nodding deferentially to Zoe in her status as guest, the black-garbed woman beckoned to Alex and addressed him in torrent of Greek.

''*Parakalo, Yaya*,'' he said after a moment. ''Please excuse me, everyone. I'll just be a minute. I have a phone call from one of our dealers in California.''

As he left the room, Zoe felt certain he'd sent an additional, unspoken directive to her. Don't try to slip out without me, *Zoe mou*, he'd warned, fixing her with the full force of his amber gaze. This time I won't rely on the Fates to find you.

Four

Perversely, she couldn't stop herself from accepting his unspoken challenge. Thanks to his father's cooperation, her business in Tarpon Springs was at an end, and she could leave at any time. Making her abrupt excuses to a surprised Stavros and the rest of the Kalandris family, she slipped out the door and almost ran to her car. A few minutes later, she was checking out of the Dolphin Inn. Her little import's tires squealed as she tore out of the parking lot.

The phone was ringing as she unlocked the door of her Tallahassee apartment. Probably it's for Carole, she told herself, putting down her bag. But she knew better than that—even before she picked up the receiver and murmured a breathless, "Hello."

Alex's voice conjured up the entire gorgeous, impossible-for-her man. "Zoe," he demanded, coming directly to the point, "why did you walk out on me that way? Weren't you well treated by my family? Is there some reason we can't be friends?"

Shielded by distance from any reproach in his matchless eyes, she still flushed at her own childish behavior. Yet though her embarrassment was flooded with regret, she knew she couldn't have acted otherwise—not without risking her hard-won independence from her Greek heritage.

"I'm...afraid you have the wrong person," she managed at last, berating herself for the untruth. "This is Carole Foster, Zoe's roommate. She's away on a business trip at the moment. May I take a message?"

There was a brief silence in which he seemed to assess the story's patent phoniness. "Sorry," he said, "but you sound very like her. Would you tell her Alex phoned? She can reach me at my home until midnight...if she wants to return my call."

He gave her a number and she found herself scribbling it on the notepad beside the phone. "I'll tell her," she promised weakly.

"Thanks. *Kalinikta.*"

She stood there briefly motionless after he broke the connection. So he knew, she acknowledged. That soft good-night in Greek was meant to tell me so.

To her surprise, hot tears were stinging her eyelids. She wasn't worried that he would embarrass her with his father or the governor by complaining of her headlong flight from his hospitality and friendship. She knew without being told that he was too much of a gentleman for that.

Instead, it was far more likely that he would let her have her way: stay out of any further negotiations that might be necessary and out of her life unless she returned his call. Since she didn't intend to do that—didn't *dare* do it, despite the haunting imprint of his mouth—she probably wouldn't see him again.

With an effort of will she crumpled the slip of paper with his phone number on it and dropped it into the wastebasket. Then, taking off her creased business suit and stepping out of her shoes, she let them fall with uncharacteristic abandon as she went into her room.

Standing before the bathroom sink a few minutes later to brush her teeth, she confronted her own rueful gaze in the mirror. Try as she would, she couldn't escape the memory of Alex's strongly modeled, faintly irregular features and light-drenched eyes that seemed able to look into her very soul.

You've finally found someone who could force you to give him everything on his own terms and then accept it with the most devastating tenderness, her inner self prodded. Forget the fact that he's Greek by accident of birth. Let him show you what it's like to be expertly and thoroughly loved.

At the very thought, a wave of gooseflesh passed over her skin. "No," she whispered. Learning to care about him would be too dangerous—a deliberate step backward into the prison of my grandmother's world.

Warning herself not to cultivate unruly fantasies, she got under the covers and turned out the light. But sleep wouldn't come and she knew it might be several hours before Carole returned from her fiancé's apartment. Bereft of any sounding board but her own confused heart, Zoe stumbled back into the living room to retrieve the scrap of paper with Alex's phone number. Smoothing it out, she laid it carefully on the night table beside her bed.

Sane reflection the next morning wouldn't let her call. There wasn't time to brood. When she arrived at the office, discussion of another assignment, this time one involving problems with a trucking union, followed closely on the heels of congratulations for a job well done. She was on her way to Jacksonville almost before she had time to repack her bags.

Her sessions with the truckers and company managers were marked by tough negotiating and emotionally charged give-and-take that claimed all her attention. It was only at night, in the plush emptiness of her expensive motel room, that she thought of ouzo and sunsets. Hugging herself, she relived again and again the sweet, unexpected assault of Alex's mouth and wondered what might have happened between them had she stayed.

When she returned home at the end of the week with a tentative agreement in hand, Carole had some surprising news. "Just your luck," her roommate remarked as Zoe dumped down her things. "You missed the most fabulous caller. Apollo came knocking on your door."

"Apollo, you say?" Startled at such an unerring description of the man she'd been trying to forget, she stared at her friend in consternation. "You don't mean Alex Kalandris, do you?"

"The same." Zoe's roommate regarded her with narrowed eyes. "And a definite prize, I might add. What's wrong with you, anyway, Zoe? He mentioned that you were forced to leave Tarpon Springs ahead of schedule before the two of you could have dinner together. You know your job is more flexible than that."

Zoe didn't bother to deny an obvious truth. "So?" she asked, feeling both flattered and defensive. "What else did he have on his mind?"

Carole shrugged. "Not much . . . he said something about returning from a business trip to Mobile and stopping by to remedy the situation."

She couldn't hide an absurd wave of pleasure.

"Zoe . . ." Carole said thoughtfully.

"Hmm?" Keeping her voice level, she bent over her suitcase.

As usual, she didn't deceive her roommate in the slightest. "Blaine Walker's a thing of the past," Carole reminded her. "It's time you started seeing someone else. This magnificent Greek you've turned up is positively charming. I hope you won't be fool enough to let him get away."

Though she was flattered that Alex had chosen to pursue their acquaintance, Zoe was stubborn in her refusal to contact him. Accordingly, Christmas was a melancholy affair. Nothing could be done about the Tarpon Springs question until after the first of the year, and there wasn't even a slim chance of their being thrown together until then. Meanwhile, the governor's staff was granted a long holiday. She moped about at loose ends, refusing to put up a tree or evince any holiday spirit. After Carole left for Georgia to visit her fiancé's parents, the apartment seemed as empty as Zoe's heart.

It was at times like those that she felt her lack of family the most. As always, she blamed the *Yaya*. Mom died partly because she had no fight left in her, Zoe asserted as she leafed through her mother's worn picture album. If *Yaya* had loved and wanted us, Mom might have had the emotional strength to battle against her illness and win remission as her doctors had hoped. We might have been baking cookies together now or shopping for family gifts.

Yet though she was in a pensive, almost bitter mood, her imaginings weren't all unhappy ones. She didn't consciously engineer it, but a man who looked very like Alex Kalandris figured repeatedly in her waking dreams. Well, she asked herself irritably as she came across a faded photograph of her parents on the porch of the Pericles Street house. Is that what you want—an old-fashioned life in the shadow of your husband's relatives? Even if you'd grown up there and married a man like Alex, you probably wouldn't be enjoying the career you have today. Doubtlessly you'd have given up on law school, anyway. The Kalandris women may seem to be on an equal footing with their men, but behind the scenes it's probably another story.

Despite such thoughts, she couldn't get the tall scion of the Kalandris family out of her mind. It was more than devotion to her job that prompted her to check several days later on the progress that was being made in drafting the sponge-exchange bill. In the back of her mind was the wildly improbable notion that she might phone Stavros to report on that progress as promised, and reach his eldest son by mistake.

She hesitated just long enough that matters were taken out of her hands. Early in the day on New Year's Eve, Alex called her again. "Zoe?" he asked in a skeptical tone, quite as if he expected her to attempt another impersonation.

But she had missed him too much for that. "Hello, Alex," she breathed, deeply affected just by the sound of his voice.

He didn't take her to task. Instead he was friendly and uncritical as he invited her to bring him up to date on the sponge-exchange project, and posed several pertinent questions.

Much too quickly she shared everything she knew. She found herself despairing that soon they'd have nothing more to talk about. If she didn't shift their conversation onto a more personal level, she guessed, it would end as pleasantly and noncommittally as it had begun.

I don't want that to happen, she admitted with reluctance. Maybe he's wrong for me, but I want to see him again. If I don't, I'm going to spend the rest of my life wondering about what might have been.

She needn't have worried that he would leave the burden of arranging things to her. "Zoe," he said, abruptly changing the subject, "we have some unfinished business, don't you think? How would you like to come down and spend New Year's with me? You wouldn't have to see your relatives or talk about the past."

Though she'd been casting about for a way to let him know how much she regretted her rude behavior, the forthright invitation caught her by surprise. "Just...come down and *stay* with you?" she faltered, blurting out the first words that came into her mind. "What will your parents think?"

She imagined him suppressing a sudden smile. "I'm sure they'd be delighted to see you," he responded dryly. "However, I don't plan on sharing your company with them. I have the privacy of my own place...and a live-in maid who can act as a chaperone, if that's important to you."

She flushed a little though he couldn't see her face. "I'm still...not sure it would be the right thing to do...."

"Why wouldn't it be? We live miles apart, which makes it a bit difficult to arrange an evening dinner date." There was a slight pause. "I suppose you could stay in a motel if you like. But I assure you...my house is much more comfortable. We can get to know each other better there."

Zoe bit her lip. The thought of sharing his home, outrageous as it still seemed, was more attractive to her than she liked to confess. Her very bones threatened to melt at the prospect, almost as helplessly as they had when he'd pulled her up against him on board his uncle's boat and impressed her body permanently with the remembered shape of his.

Nonetheless, she hardly knew him. Every scruple in her cried out that it would be wrong to do what he was suggesting. Every unsoothed hurt pleaded with her to be wary, even while she yearned for the excitement of seeing him again. He's not asking you to marry him, she reminded herself sharply, just to spend a few days in his company. And he's made it clear that nights in his bed aren't part of the bargain—unless you want them to be. You won't be condemned to the life your mother led if you say yes.

"Well?" he prompted in that low, not-quite-accented voice that could so easily breach her defenses. "Are you going to let your spontaneous Greek self decide? Or must I swoop down on you like Poseidon on poor Anclote and carry you away?"

His reference to the story he'd told her that night beside the river pushed her past hesitation. To accede to his wishes might end in worse than sorrow, but life stretched bleak and uninviting without the chance to be with him again, even if only for a little while.

"All right, Alex," she agreed, swayed by the allure of him. "I'm probably crazy to do it, but I'll come down for a few days. The truth is, I've been thinking of you, too."

On her way to Tarpon Springs later that morning, Zoe felt more than a little foolish for reversing herself. *You should have told him no,* her more conservative side insisted. *You can still turn back, call him from the nearest pay phone.*

Instead she kept driving straight ahead, her thoughts on fire with the possibilities of what they could share. Almost before she realized it, she was negotiating the narrow streets of the small coastal town where she'd been born and making a right at Saint Nicholas Cathedral. Taking the road that wound along the bayou, she turned again just before reaching the little bridge, as Alex had directed. There were butterflies in her stomach as she parked in the gravel lot at the Kalandris boatyard. Wondering if she looked all right in her nubby yellow silk slacks and sweater, she ran her fingers through tousled curls as she made her way past a large open shed where men were layering fiberglass on the unfinished hull of a boat.

Moments later she was hesitantly pushing open his office door. A reception area littered with blueprints and sales literature and color photographs of sailing yachts first met her eye. Then memory paled as she saw him through the glass partition that delineated his private work area. Dressed in jeans and a turtleneck, he was speaking to someone whose back was turned.

And there was no doubt about it this time: to her he was the most special man in all the world.

Transfixed, she stared at him through the dusty pane, memorizing his rugged good looks, stunning build and the innate passion and vitality he unconsciously betrayed with his every movement.

Then he felt her eyes on him and glanced in her direction, flashing her that heartbreaking smile. It wasn't difficult to read him through the glass. "Zoe!" he said, cutting short his conversation.

She trembled a little as he came out and stopped just short of taking her into his arms. Instead he fastened his hands with casual possession on her shoulders, his fingers learning their shape through the sweater's luxurious texture.

"I'm so glad you've come, *krysi mou*," he told her, looking at her with an expression of such delight that she could feel the warmth of it down to her toes.

He had called her his golden one. "So am I, Alex," she whispered.

A small silence rested between them. She could feel him sharing her surprise that they were actually together again. All the danger she had imagined and more was present, there in topaz depths and the pressure of his firm yet sensual touch. The last thing she wanted now was to run from it. Instead she longed to place herself utterly in his keeping.

Lord of the lyre and Zeus's best-loved son, she thought, giving way to the pull of him. I could fall in love with you.

Gradually she became aware that the man he'd been speaking to earlier had come out of the office. Alex appeared to give himself a mental shake. "Zoe, this is Georgiou Pappadapoulos, my foreman, who also helps with the design," he said, a muscle working alongside his mouth. "We're shutting down early today, Georgiou . . . tell the crew."

With a few polite words to her, Georgiou went out. They were alone. Her pulse quickened as she thought Alex might kiss her; the idea seemed fleetingly to express itself in his beautiful eyes. In the next moment he appeared to decide against it, though she went on imagining how his tongue would tease her lips apart.

"So you took my advice and gave your Greek self the upper hand," he teased, breaking the spell only a little. "How would you like to see my operation here before we go?"

Mutely she nodded her assent. His hand on her arm, he led her out into the brilliant sunlight. Word about the boatyard shutting down early had spread quickly, Zoe saw. The men who crafted the Kalandris yachts were already departing with car keys and lunch pails in hand. Several of them called out what might be a New Year's wish, adding a few rapid-fire comments in Greek she couldn't understand. Most of them gave her appreciative smiles.

For the space of several seconds, Zoe wondered if she should have come. She knew that news traveled with astonishing speed in Tarpon Springs. By evening, it would be common knowledge that Alex Kalandris had a female houseguest. Before much longer, everyone would know that houseguest's name and history, including her own grandmother.

A quick glance at him righted her resolve. What does it matter if *Yaya* finds out, compared with this chance to share his company, she thought, returning Alex's smile. What you're doing won't interfere with your mission for the governor, and you certainly don't plan to visit *Yaya* before you go.

She managed to forget her scruples entirely as Alex began his tour by showing her how the hulls of his yachts were bonded by building up layer after layer of fiberglass for lightness and strength. In passing, he cautioned her not to let any of the loose fiberglass strands that lay scattered on the floor like angel hair get caught in her open-toed sandals. "I wouldn't want to find myself extracting little pieces of it from your pretty toes," he told her. "Believe me, this stuff hurts."

As he showed her around, he began to speak on a more personal level, about his own past and about his grandfather, who had learned boat-building skills as a young man in Greek ports off the Turkish coast.

"I spent hours down here with him as a boy," he said, his voice warm with remembered affection. "Every chance I got...learning how the wooden prototypes were made and how to build a boat that would be worthy on the water. I came to love the smooth feel of rubbed teak and the crisp canvas of the sails...even that acrid, chemical smell of the chop, or fiberglass binder.

"Because I was the eldest, my father wanted and expected me to go to law school one day... partly to live out the American dream as he saw it, I suppose, and partly to give our family the advantages of a partisan counsel. Being a good son, I wanted to please him. And I admit to a fondness for the law, despite what I told you several weeks ago.

"It's just that it never captured my imagination. While I was still an undergraduate, I took courses in nautical engineering whenever I could. And when I came back here with my law degree, I knew what I really wanted to do. Boats are in my blood and probably in my soul. I tend to lose myself in creating them, just as my grandfather did."

Keenly aware of him as they made a leisurely circuit of the cabinetmakers' shop, the sail room and the grinders' shed, Zoe realized that he had offered her a genuine glimpse of his private self. In her limited experience, men talked a lot about themselves and revealed very little. A place that had been lonely for that kind of intimacy warmed within her even as she guessed there'd be no hiding from his openness. Every secret, she acknowledged, and complete trust—that's what he'll expect if and when we make love.

"*I* wanted very much to become a lawyer," she admitted, belatedly offering him a bit of herself in return.

One dark brow quirked a little. "Why didn't you, then?"

"The money wasn't there."

"I'm sorry to hear it. But... that's how it is sometimes. You can still go after it when the time is right, don't you suppose?"

More than a little startled, Zoe considered his words with a thoughtful expression. For a long time she had blamed *Yaya* for most of the disappointments in her life, including the tight budget that had made law school an impossibility. Now she realized her lack of family support didn't need to matter. Though she'd refused any help from Blaine, she'd worked hard and saved her money. She had a nest egg that could be put to whatever purpose she chose.

But it had taken Alex's simple statement of fact to make her realize her own responsibility in the matter.

"Maybe I will, Alex," she told him, turning the thought around in her mind. "Maybe I just will."

"Good." Lightly he squeezed her shoulder.

A few minutes later they halted beside a nearly completed sailing yacht out in the yard. It was cradled in an electronic hoist so that the finishing touches could be put to its hull as well as to its fittings and cabinetwork. The craft's two masts, the main and the mizzen, were already stepped in place.

Alex followed her admiring look. "Want to climb up and see her?" he asked, indicating the metal equivalent of a rope ladder that to her seemed exclusively designed for mountain goats or sailors.

"If you'll give me a hand."

"Nice shape," he noted a moment later as he steadied her ascent from behind. Then, at her swift, comically deploring look, he laughed aloud, a warm and completely masculine sound. "I say what I think. I can't help it," he shrugged as she stepped ahead of him into the sloop's sleek, exquisitely appointed cabin. "Anyhow, 'nice shape' is also the name of my own sloop. I call her *Eidothea* in Greek. More exactly translated, that means 'she of the goddesslike form.' Tomorrow, if you like, we'll take her out on the water."

When they had finished their inspection, Alex insisted on transferring her luggage to his Mercedes. "We keep the gate locked, and your car will be safe here over the holiday," he said, courteously settling her against the automobile's rich leather upholstery.

She watched as he got behind the wheel and inserted his key into the ignition. But he didn't start the engine just yet. Instead he turned to her, a message she'd read earlier back with heart-stopping intensity in his eyes.

"Now that I have you safely in my keeping, I want to kiss you again, my beautiful girl," he told her unexpectedly.

She was disarmed by the soft declaration. Tentatively, as if he knew there was a great deal of hesitation still in her, he slipped one hand around to the back of her neck and tangled his fingers in the short curls at her nape. With the other hand he tilted her chin to his.

Blood pounded dizzily in her ears even before the first tenuous brush of his mouth sent fire racing along her veins. The scent of him and the taste, remembered so many times since she'd experienced them last, overruled any objection. She moved into his embrace as heedlessly as someone might step off a precipice if they believed they could fly. With a little gesture of abandon and trust, she slipped her arms around his neck. Her lips parted beneath his, inviting him to ravage her mouth's moist recesses.

"Ah, Zoe," he whispered, the words muffled against her as he deepened his kiss.

Swift stabs of pleasure and desire rendered her helpless at the invasion of his tongue as he frankly and sensually probed to take full possession. She shook with a heated chill as his hand slipped beneath her sweater to lay claim to the smooth skin of her back and draw her more closely into his embrace. Her breasts were pinned against his chest, their nipples erect and aching. Hard against her knee, his thigh attested to his superb conditioning for the act of love.

But it was more than just his demand and his hardness that made her inner reaches warm and expand

and deepen in preparation for surrender. Sweetly
mauling hers, his mouth communicated an overwhel-
ing generosity of spirit that she'd known only once
before—in his arms. Here's a man, it promised, who
could enjoy you the way you've always wanted to be
enjoyed, with both tenderness and lust.

I could be a well for him, she thought in amazement. As deep as the earth and as open as he might
require.

Then it was over. Her breath came in a ragged little
gasp as gently he drew apart.

"Zoe, Zoe, you're inviting me to do much more
than kiss you, don't you know that?" he asked.

"Yes," she admitted, wondering at the half-guilty
look she had surprised on his face.

A moment later she knew its cause. "I have a
confession to make," he added, leaning back and
lighting a cigarette with a little whoosh of flame. "This
morning on the phone, I swear I told you the truth.
But the chaperone I promised you won't be available.
My housekeeper had to go to Tampa to be with her
grandson. His mother went into early labor this
afternoon."

Five

They would be alone. Slowly the full implication of what he was saying took shape in her mind. She couldn't guess how her pupils dilated at the notion, seeming to swallow up the velvety brown irises that surrounded them.

"I'm sorry," he said after a minute with a little shake of his head. "I should have told you before transferring all your luggage to my car. If you'd rather stay in a motel, after all, I'd be more than happy to foot the bill...."

"No," she whispered.

We'll be lovers now, she added silently, unless I can stop myself. And I don't even want to think about what the consequences of that will be. I should back away while I still have a chance.

"No, you don't want to stay in a motel?" he asked, watching the play of emotions on her face. "Or no, you won't allow me to pay?"

He hadn't even admitted the possibility that she might just go. Zoe took a deep breath. "The motel won't be necessary," she told him. "We're both adults and I trust your hospitality. Besides I'm a formerly married woman. I should be able to handle myself with a man."

The look he gave her was more ambivalent than she had expected. Though his pleasure that she would stay with him was unmistakable, she sensed he hadn't quite liked the rest of her statement. I wonder if he thinks I'm making up my marriage, she thought. Or if he was hoping I'd jump at the chance to be alone with him.

He didn't enlighten her. "Let's go, then," he said in a casual tone as he backed out of the parking space.

Alex's house faced the Gulf of Mexico from a grove of cedars and shaggy dark green pines. Modern, angular and finished in gleaming white stucco to reflect the light, it suggested but didn't imitate what she knew of Aegean architecture.

She caught her breath at the rightness of it for him as they went inside. Open and airy beneath heavily beamed ceilings, the rooms had been designed for a warm climate with large windows and thick, roughly stuccoed walls, cool terra-cotta floors. Hand-woven rugs in striped wool, and shaggy, luxurious *flokatis* of ivory-colored sheep's wool softened their hard surfaces, as did oversize upholstered pieces in natural fabrics. She noted a collection of handmade pottery set into tiled niches in the walls. The lovely worn patina of several antique pieces in what was probably olive wood made a striking textural contrast.

Beyond a curved archway, she glimpsed his sleek, up-to-the-minute kitchen, where wicker baskets and copper pots hung from the ceiling. More copper utensils, hand hammered and looking as if they'd been acquired in a street market, hung beside the great room's hearth. A scattering of handloomed pillows invited fire gazers to stretch out at their ease.

Through an uncurtained wall of windows, she saw a pair of white canvas slingback chairs, placed under a rustic bougainvillea arbor to overlook the expanse of the Gulf as it melted into the horizon.

"Will it do?" he asked, smiling as he continued to hold her luggage.

"Admirably," she said.

Just imagine living here, she enjoined herself. Think how it would be to wake up in this tranquil, sunlit world, breakfast in those canvas chairs with Alex, to remember passion against cool sheets whenever your eyes happened to meet. The joy of it would be all you could bear—if there wasn't an old-world social structure waiting beyond these walls to claim him.

She was slightly pensive as he led her to a guest bedroom with the same breathtaking view, this time framed by typically Greek fringed open-worked curtains. You're tempting fate, she thought, as she washed up and reapplied her makeup, then slipped into diaphanous sapphire-blue lounging pajamas. She'd bought them her last afternoon in Jacksonville with him in mind.

But her mood didn't last. Alex, who had changed into gray wool trousers and a white shirt that contrasted with his tan, was popping a champagne cork when she emerged. "It's nearly five o'clock already," he reminded her. "Time to start celebrating the New Year . . . and our friendship. I intend that both get off to a beautiful start."

Time poured out like honey that evening as Alex grilled steaks and prepared a salad with all the expertise of a practiced chef. "They say most Greeks have a restaurant owner somewhere in their family tree," he said with a laugh, handing her a piece of watercress to taste as he anointed the salad liberally with ground pepper, olive oil and lemon. "I try not to let Angelika know I'm such a good cook. She's from the old school, you understand. She prefers to think that men are helpless in the kitchen."

By the time they were ready to eat, the sun had gone down and they closed the patio doors against the rapidly cooling night air. To her delight, Alex lit a fire and they carried in their plates to picnic with more champagne among the pillows by the hearth.

Though Zoe ate ravenously, the alcohol seemed to go more quickly than usual to her head. She was beginning to feel slightly dizzy by the time Alex took their plates back to the kitchen and returned with a small *vasilopita*, or New Year's cake, his housekeeper had baked for them early that morning. As if by prearrangement, he cut her the exact piece that had been embedded with a tiny coin.

From her childhood, she remembered that the coin signified luck in the coming year. "Make a wish," he instructed, his eyes gleaming at her enjoyment. "But don't tell me what it is . . . unless you want me to take a hand in its fulfillment."

I don't dare wish for what I'd really like, Zoe thought. Sated and a little tipsy, she leaned back against the cushions to watch as he reached for one of the fireplace matches and lit a cigarette. Visually she traced his features in the shifting light—the strong, slightly aquiline nose and wide, generous mouth, little laugh lines that crinkled beside his eyes.

Try as she would, she couldn't seem to keep her gaze from roving lower to acquaint itself with the whole wonderfully made length of his body. All man and all mine if I want him—at least for tonight, she guessed, noting his trim, hard midsection and narrow thighs.

"What would you be doing if I weren't here?" she asked, shutting out all conscious consideration of such enticing possibilities.

He shrugged. "Oh, I suppose I'd be with my family and friends at Zorba's, a local nightclub, dancing and drinking and throwing away money by the handful."

"Literally?"

"Sure. I don't suppose you remember those parties where the men get up and try to outdance one another. Everyone, including his competitor, throws money at the dancer who is most admired, so that it flutters all over the floor to be trampled in the dust."

In truth, she did vaguely recall such scenes in the distant past. "Just the men dance?" she asked, frowning a little.

He shook his head. "No, everybody...women, children, old people, lovers...sometimes all in one big line that snakes around and around the room."

Zoe had to admit that the idea had a certain appeal. "Are you sorry...that you're not there, celebrating tonight?" she asked.

"Not when I have you in my house."

For a moment his eyes narrowed, and she could read a deep sexuality in them, controlled yet so powerful that she caught her breath. "Maybe someday, if the past loses its hold on you a little, we'll dance at Zorba's together," he added quietly, getting to his feet.

She thought he might pull her up beside him. Instead he switched off the stereo, and returned with an instrument very similar to a hammered dulcimer and sat down beside her. "As part of your reeducation in Greek ways, I'll teach you about the *sandouri*," he said.

The tune he chose was both plaintive and sweet, an eastern Mediterranean folk song that might have come down to them from ancient times. Charmed by his many facets and influenced more than she realized by all the champagne, Zoe laid her hand lightly on his knee as she watched his expert fingering.

If she'd glanced up just then, she'd have realized he was hardly immune to the gesture. "Here, let me show you how it's done," he offered, putting one arm around her and positioning her fingers on the strings.

She managed to pick out just a few discordant notes before giving up with a laugh.

"Too much bubbly," he observed, lowering his mouth to nuzzle softly at her neck.

The casual kiss sent little shivers of longing down her spine. "You'll have to give me a lot more to drink than that if you want to make a musician of me," she joked, deliberately taking another sip. "There aren't any musicians on my family tree, Greek or otherwise."

Alex shook his head. "You're wrong...champagne doesn't improve any activity requiring fine motor skills or heightened concentration and that includes love-making.''

With one decisive hand, he took the glass from her fingers and set it beside the *sandouri* on the hearth. His other was on her breast, touching and defining one hardening nipple through her top's gauzy cotton fabric.

"I had intended taking more time with you, my beautiful girl," he warned. "But I've been wanting you too long. If you don't stop me, I'm going to make love to you."

Her body was on his side. At his words, white-hot currents shot from her sensitized bud to the very core of her desire, causing it to throb with a need only he could assuage. Unable to speak, she leaned back against him and offered up her mouth.

His mouth suddenly covered hers. His hands took firm possession of both her breasts, sending twin currents of need plunging through her body. Though they were covered by a barrier of fabric, her nipples began to ache for the pull of his mouth.

Lost to everything but him, she dared to taste profoundly of him in return, caressing his roughly questing tongue with her own.

For him, her forthright response was clearly a goad. "Zoe, my dove, can you know how much I want you?" he asked, abandoning her mouth for the warm curve of her shoulder.

"I know how much I want you."

Somehow she found herself on her knees, there on the *flokati* rug in the firelight. Alex was removing her tunic and she was raising her arms to help. A moment later, he was unhooking her bra.

Her soft, full breasts spilled out into his hands like ripe fruit and she moaned a little at the sensation.

"Beautiful, oh, so beautiful," he murmured, running the tips of his fingers over her swollen curves. "Even more lovely than I imagined them...."

The next minute he was unbuttoning his shirt with one hand, as with the other he pushed gently at one rosy bud with his thumb. Zoe thought she would go mad with wanting. Just the sight of his bare torso, bronze from the sun and so well muscled it might have been sculpted by Praxiteles, made the ache of longing deepen within her body.

Breathlessly she caressed him in turn, exploring the coarse texture of his chest hair with her fingertips and drawing tiny whorls around his flat male nipples so that a wave of gooseflesh passed over his skin.

"Yes, touch me, darling. I want you to," he urged, shutting his eyes momentarily at what must be small stabs of pleasure similar to her own.

Emboldened, she lowered her head to place a series of tiny, blunt kisses on his chest. The texture of his dark hair was like an aphrodisiac. Smoothing the long muscles of his back, her hands dared to dip beneath the waistband of his slacks and touch the hard curve of his upper buttocks.

In response, he thrust himself up against her, so that she could feel his hardness and heat. Then he was inviting her to lie back against the cushions and covering her with his body, seeking out one breast to flick its nipple back and forth against his tongue. As she cradled his head against her, he took the nipple fully into his mouth and began to suck with wet, vigorous abandon, not bothering to quiet the sound.

Little tremors shook her. Momentarily raising his head to view her pleasure, he licked and tugged at her other breast in turn, as if he would draw all the sweetness from her body. Overcome with what he was making her feel, and shaken, too, just at the sight of him, so tanned and masculine as he mouthed her ivory swell, Zoe urged him on with her hands.

I want you inside me, she silently begged in the erotic shorthand of touch. You...filling me to the depths so that we're like one person, without even the smallest empty place between us.

With the thought came her first premonition of the kind of commitment he might evoke. Briefly she was able to push it aside. Her breasts gleamed damp from his mouth as he slid her sapphire trousers down over her hips and removed the final barrier of her bikini panties. Yet the caveat came to mind more compellingly as his hands and mouth moved over her thighs.

You'll learn to love him, she realized with stunning clarity—not just for tonight or tomorrow, but for a lifetime. And it would be a disaster, because you can't accept his world.

Unaware of the conflict in her heart, Alex removed his trousers and undershorts to reveal his need. Her lips parted at the hard male beauty of him. Greedily her gaze stroked down his thighs, longing to feel those muscles bunch as he entered to claim her.

"Don't hold anything back from me," he whispered, straddling her. "I want to put my mouth everywhere...make you mindless with pleasure before I take my fill."

It was what she wanted, too, just to forget the problems of ethnic origin and place and open her body to him, be both Aphrodite and mother goddess to this

glorious man. But she couldn't allow it to happen—
not now, and maybe not ever.

"No, Alex. *No*."

The words seemed torn from some deep and childlike part of her even as her woman's body wanted to
strangle them in her throat. With a little moan of distress, she struggled to be free, tears wetting her cheeks
as he caught her by the shoulders.

"Zoe?" he asked in astonishment and confusion.
"What's the matter, sweetheart? How have I hurt
you?"

"You haven't. Oh, Alex...I'm sorry to be such a
fool."

For several seconds he simply held her, demanding
nothing and trying, she guessed, to understand.
"Please," he said at last. "I know you wanted what
was happening as much as I. Tell me why we can't
make love."

She was still naked in his arms and suddenly her
position seemed ludicrous, almost humiliating. Pushing him away, she fumbled about for her clothing.

"Here. Take my shirt."

"I'd prefer it if you were angry with me," she said,
turning her face away as he helped her into the sleeves
and buttoned several buttons.

"Well, I'm not. I'd just rather know what's
wrong."

Haltingly then, she tried to explain. "You're right,
I wanted you," she admitted. "More than I've ever
wanted any man. It's just that...I could learn to care
for you. I know you never asked me to and that we've
only known each other a little while.

"But it's true, all the same. And I'm terrified because you're Greek. I...don't want to step back into

the past, find myself caught in the world my mother hated...."

The confession had laid bare her very soul. He accepted it in silence, and she thought he would be angry with her after all. Then he got to his feet and pulled on his pants, his eyes not leaving her face.

"The past is dead," he told her gently, drawing her up beside him. "And we're two different people, Zoe, who live in a different time. If you'll give me half a chance, maybe I can show you that."

More tears spilled as he led her off to his beautifully appointed guest room and tucked her in beneath a deep, soft coverlet.

"Too much champagne," he repeated, leaning over to brush her forehead with just the trace of a kiss. "Sleep well. Things will look different in the morning."

It was only later, when the midnight bells and firecrackers went off in the distance, that she roused from a restless slumber to understand fully what his forbearance had cost. From her bedroom window, she saw Alex, bundled in a jacket and outlined against the silvery Gulf water. The firefly glow of his cigarette stabbed at the dark.

Morning came, and with it a light fog. Alex tapped at her door and then entered, carrying a breakfast tray. As if to banish all thought of his Greek heritage, he had laden it with hearty American fare—eggs, sausage, coffee and orange juice and tiny, crisp rolls.

Rubbing the sleep from her eyes, she realized she was still wearing his shirt, and wondered if it would remind him of the previous night's fiasco.

If it did he gave no sign. "Eat," he ordered good-
naturedly, sitting down on the bed beside her as if such
intimacy were commonplace between them. "This fog
will lift by ten o'clock. I hope you brought a warm
sweater or a jacket. It's going to be cool out there today on the water."

Though smaller, the *Eidothea* was possibly more
beautiful than the sloop she'd seen the day before in
the Kalandris boatyard. Following his instructions
with the lines, she helped him put out into the channel and then came to sit nearby as he set sail before the
brisk north wind toward Saint Joseph Sound. In-
stinctively she could feel his pleasure in the craft's trim
response, his appreciation of her carefully engineered
elegance as she sliced through the water.

He was right, she thought, watching the breeze blow
through his hair and the squint lines crinkle up beside
his golden eyes. Boats do have a living spirit. Now I
understand why they mean so much to him.

As they came about and tacked northward again, he
raised his voice above the sound of the spray to tell her
the story behind the sloop's name. "Eidothea was a
nymph, the daughter of Proteus, the sea god," he explained. "Proteus alone could tell King Menelaus how
to break Athene's adverse spell on his return voyage
from the Trojan War. The nymph graciously advised
him how to capture her father and so secure a south-
erly breeze."

Sometime later they anchored on the leeward side of
Anclote Key. They were near the lighthouse and would
be out of the wind. For a while they rocked gently on
the swells, drinking the coffee he'd brought in a ther-
mos and sharing bits and pieces of their separate pasts.

Hugging herself in the chilly, intermittent sunshine, Zoe told him what she could of her parents. She added only few words about her grandmother; the *Yaya* was still difficult for her to talk about. In response to his prodding, she even spoke briefly of her failed marriage and the fact that Blaine meant nothing to her now. He seemed satisfied at her words. *Probably he realizes that the trouble between us doesn't originate from there,* she thought.

In return, Alex talked about his parents, too—warmly, as she had guessed he would—and told her a little more about the time he'd been sent to Greece in his late twenties to find a wife.

"I'd been there only once before, as a boy with my grandfather," he said, "and I was delighted at the chance to return. But in truth I never expected my mission to be accomplished, and ultimately I came back alone. You see, I wanted someone who was born here and understood new ways as well as old ones...."

She didn't comment. "The main problem, though," he added, "was much simpler than that. I just didn't find anyone with whom I could fall in love."

Zoe held out her mug for a refill of coffee. "Wasn't your father disappointed?"

He shrugged. "I imagine he was...for a while. When Kon's turn came, he married a local girl who was a friend of the family. And it appears that Adonis will do the same. Now, I think, my father would be happy if I'd settle down with any suitable woman...Greek or otherwise...and give him the grandchildren he wants."

Fearing that despite her denial of him the night before she wanted to be that woman, Zoe longed to ask if he planned to grant his father's wish. She had the feeling that he sensed both her question and her unwillingness to broach it.

Abruptly he began to reel in the anchor. "Time for another quick run down the bay before the weather changes," he said, licking his finger and holding it up to the shifting breeze. "I think we're going to have fog again before very long."

As they ran part of the way back toward Honeymoon Island, they could see the fog approaching. Slowly it advanced toward them like a gray curtain across the water.

"We should have started back sooner," Alex admitted, bringing them about. "It's moving in much faster than I thought."

The thick gray mist caught them in its eerie silence before they had quite reached the channel. With the dying down of the breeze came a penetrating cold that made Zoe shiver in her heavy fuchsia-and-purple sweater.

"Here," said Alex, throwing her a slicker. "I'd tell you to go below, but unfortunately I need you to help with the lines. Stay warm if you can while I try to find the markers."

For what seemed an eternity they groped about in a muffled, pewter-colored world until Alex located the channel entrance. Her hands were like ice, her nose red and her teeth chattering by the time they tied up in the little harbor. The cold seemed to have seeped into her very bones.

Bundling her into his car, Alex put his jacket over her like a blanket and whisked her back at top speed to his house for what he said was a mandatory hot shower and whiskey drink.

"I can't have you coming down with a cold," he insisted, a protective arm about her shoulders as he led her to the larger, more luxurious shower in his personal bath. Turning on the water for her, he adjusted the temperature. "Take off your clothes and get inside," he added. "I'll be back with your drink in a moment."

Gradually the warmth of the spray in his fieldstone shower penetrated to her bones. Her chilled lungs breathed in the steamy air with gratitude as her body relaxed and quieted, began to glow pink with the heat.

She was still standing there with the water streaming down around her when he came back into the bathroom again; faintly she could see the shape of him through the frosted glass.

"I have your dirnk, *krysi mou*," he said, an unmistakable roughness catching at his voice. "If you like, I'll open the door a little and put it in your hand."

Softly she gave her assent.

He slid the glass panel ajar. His arm, muscled and gleaming in the wet, reached in to secure a steaming pottery mug in her grasp. "Careful," he warned, withdrawing again. "It's hot. I don't want you scalding your lovely mouth."

Thanking him, she grimaced a little at the whiskey's strength, though its honeyed warmth felt wonderful as it traveled down her throat. He didn't leave again, as she'd expected. When he'd handed her the toddy, she'd noticed he wasn't wearing a shirt. Isn't he cold, she wondered distractedly, even as something in her yearned to run her hands over those beautifully sculpted shoulders.

"Better, Zoe?" he asked, the same sweet roughness in his voice.

"Yes," she whispered.

"Stay there a little while."

Briefly she shut her eyes. For some reason she remembered the myth he had spun for her that first night beside the river. "Tell me a story, then," she asked, guessing where it might lead. "The way you did once before."

Though his image was blurred by the rippled glass and all the steam, she could see him lean back against the sink, a tall, bronzed shape in what were probably dry jeans.

For a moment he didn't say anything. Then, "Imagine we're in Greece, on the slope of Mount Parnassos, near Delphi," he directed. "It's spring, and there's been more than the usual rain. You, Zoe, are a nymph who has come to bathe in a sunlit torrent, unaware that Apollo has singled you out for his favor...."

Perhaps not trusting himself to speak further, he fell silent.

If she shivered, this time it wasn't with cold. In some irrational part of herself, she almost believed that he was a god, come to pleasure her and sow her with his hero's seed. How shall I fight it, she wondered, weakening with her need for him. How deny what we both want, with my puny mortal strength?

"What...what happens next?" she dared to prompt him.

"That's up to you, my beautiful girl."

Stepping nearer, he laid hold of the shower door handle. Unsteadily she turned off the faucets and set the mug down at her feet, beside the drain. "Please..." she asked, her words scarcely above a whisper, "would you mind getting me a towel?"

Six

Naked and dripping, she emerged into the white terry bath sheet he held. He wrapped it around her and turned her to face him, his arms holding her fast. Their gaze met and held, and there was no mistaking the lust in his tawny eyes, but that wasn't the only emotion she could discern there. Clearly visible were enough admiration and affection to break the heart.

"I don't think I could bear it, *Zoe mou*, if we started this again and didn't finish," he told her, smoothing a stray curl back from her forehead.

It was a moment for truth, and the only truth she knew was her strong love for him, a love that had grown despite her unwillingness, without even the nourishment of surrender.

It was a love that would survive, even if their time together could not. I'll have to take the consequences, she decided, because I won't deny him again.

Something generous and improvisational seemed to break free in her at the thought. Standing on tiptoe, she let the bath sheet fall from her body. Without understanding how it had happened, she had become the nymph of his sunlit chronicle, eager and wanton, completely ready to pleasure her lord.

Eyes narrowed and head thrown back a little, she rubbed her hardened nipples across the coarse, dark mat that covered his chest. "That won't happen," she promised, her arms encircling him. "I can't do without you, either, darling... not any more."

With a half-mute sound that might have been a Greek endearment, he swept her up in his arms. Together they stared into the steam-clouded mirror, caught by their own blurred reflection. She went weak at the sight of him, so tanned and broad shouldered, with his legs braced apart and his dark head bent to her golden one, she all blush and ivory as he held her against his chest. Though they hadn't really been intimate since the night before, the mouth of the woman in the mirror looked as if it had recently been bruised with kisses.

"Oh, Alex..." she whispered.

"I know, precious girl. Look and remember how it is with us the first time we make love."

Burrowing against the skin scent of his neck, she let him carry her off to his big bed. After the brightly lit bath, the room where he slept was like a cave, dark and welcoming. Alex loomed over her in the shadows, one knee placed between her legs. The tightness of the front of his jeans told her how much he wanted her.

But he didn't finish undressing the way she wanted him to. Instead he simply looked at her, as if committing to memory every lush curve and vulnerable hollow.

How beautiful he is and how I want him, she thought, reaching up to smooth the shape of his shoulders. Just the dear, hard bulk of him, his confident and tender masculine self. I long to make him laugh and weep and burn out of control for me, feel his movement inside my body.

But she knew he wouldn't rush to consummation. Only the night before he'd told her how he would take her, prostrating her with pleasure before indulging his need. Though she ached for completion, she awaited him like a field, yearning toward the plow yet still with anticipation.

All instinct, fully the Greek self he'd drawn so effortlessly from her psyche, she let her thighs part. "I've wanted you like this," she confessed, "from the first moment I saw you."

"As I've wanted you, sweet Zoe . . . just to fuse myself to the center of your delight."

Time fell away and space, and with them all her reasons not to have him. She moaned a little as he lowered his head to kiss her flat stomach and the little hollows beside her pelvic bones. Then his face was hidden against the coarse tuft of bronze-gold hair that covered her most intimate places. For one breathless moment she tensed, but she didn't have any real doubt that he would find her. Unerringly he located the secret mound of her desire and began to taste and touch her as if she were a banquet for the gods.

Delighted and a little shocked at the slow intimacy Alex had so naturally initiated, she clutched his dark head to her body. The warm, flooding sensation that engulfed her throbbed and pulsed, centering at its source and yet affecting her everywhere.

Unexpectedly his tongue entered her depths, and she cried out from the sheer exquisite pleasure of it. But it was the steady, moist friction he applied to her need that made the pulsing there mount into wave after wave of sensation. Each wave seemed to crest and dip only to break higher still, until she quivered like a bowstring, pulled back so tightly it must break.

"Alex..." she pleaded, her breath coming in little gasps as she moved against the pillows. "I want you inside me...oh, please...."

Raising his damp face, he caressed her with his hand. "Just let it happen," he encouraged, uncompromising and tender. "We'll come back to it together, I promise you."

Moments later, she was beyond recall, snatched up in a spiral of pleasure so intense she half rose from the bed to meet him. Helplessly she gave way to little shudders of ecstasy. All the warmth that had seemed concentrated in that upward spiral was abruptly released, and it permeated her body; her cheeks flushed and a prickle of sweat stood out on her forehead.

A deep sigh escaped her as she sank back against the pillows. His hands were stroking down her body. Little shivers, echoes of spent passion, mingled with the pleasant, aching sensation that had settled in her thighs. She let herself drift free from all moorings but him, content just to lie there in his arms.

"It was never...like *that* before," she acknowledged finally, wanting to pay him the tribute he deserved. "Never so complete."

"Ah, Zoe...." He kissed her mouth. "You please me so."

Looking at him with love, she realized to her sudden dismay that he was still partially clothed. "But Alex, you didn't..." she protested, amazed and shamed that she had so forgotten him.

He shook his head. "Rest, darling. Feel the last quiver of delight."

"No. I want you inside me...now."

Stubbornly she groped for the closure on his waistband and snapped it open. Metal rasped on metal as his zipper parted. Crisp and wiry, his body hair brushed against her fingers as she pulled the heavily stitched denim down over his thighs.

Giving in to her demand, Alex removed his jeans the rest of the way and thrust them aside. "Certain you're ready for me, sweet girl?" he asked, his hands awakening her to fresh tinglings of desire.

"Yes," she whispered. "Oh, yes, my love."

Without intending to, she had spoken to him in Greek, using words she'd heard her parents say to each other when she had been a child. Replying in the same tongue with a phrase she didn't fully understand, he moved into her embrace. For a moment she felt his hard, expectant seeking against the soft, private places he had already made his own. Then he found her and was moving inside her to claim her in the most complete way possible. Conversely, she had all of him as he filled her and then remained motionless, struggling to regain control.

She felt no violation, as she had sometimes with Blaine. Instead she was blazingly complete, joined to a man who could make her soar outside the limits of herself. Inside her, his presence kindled a hot, diffuse glow that was somehow even better than the sharp pleasure of his mouth. Inexorably it spread and deepened as he began to move, until the power of it was almost more than she could bear.

They had needed each other too much for it to last. This time the letting go was so profound that it shook her to her soul. *"Oh...oh...oh..."* she cried, her eyes shut tight as they rocked together, clinging and shuddering and then collapsing in each other's arms. Tears wet her cheeks and his weight on her was pure delight as she supported it, still circling him with her knees and arms. Her whole being felt drained and deliciously spent, as if a massive electric current had discharged to relax every muscle and nerve ending and bone.

"It's really something, isn't it, the kind of fire we can make together?" he asked after some minutes, rolling off her and drawing her head back against his shoulder.

"Really something." Breathing in his scent, she luxuriated in the feel of his skin beneath her cheek. A short time later, she had drifted off to sleep with him in the silvery afternoon.

They awoke starving. Any slight awkwardness she might have felt at finding herself naked in his bed was quickly disposed of by his blunt, approving kisses. Viewing the exotic new texture of their relationship through his eyes, she watched with unashamed interest as he put on his jeans again and then let him touch her lovingly as he wrapped her in a terry robe from his closet.

She knew as they heated and ate a *pastitso* casserole left by the housekeeper, Angelika, that she wouldn't be going back to Tallahassee that evening as planned. Instead she deliberately let the hours slip away while she cuddled with him on his couch, tracing with him in travel books the trip he'd told her about on the boat.

I'm going to spend this night with him, she thought, and not worry about tomorrow. Listen to his tales of bare, rocky islets and wildflowers and donkey bells, imagine myself by his side on brilliant terraces overlooking the sea. I can always call the office in the morning and tell them I've been detained.

Their joining that night was wild and free and even sweeter than what she had experienced that afternoon. No questions about whether they would have each other remained to be asked or answered. Relaxed and unself-conscious, they wrestled lovingly against the sheets, giving to each other from the heart.

How I love him, Zoe thought afterward as his toes stroked one sensitive sole with leisurely affection. We could move closer with each shared memory and never exhaust the possibilities. Unwilling to look beyond the moment, she realized that she felt safer and happier with this superlative man than she'd ever felt in her life.

Light was flooding his big bedroom the next morning when someone knocked shortly and then opened the door without waiting for a response. "*Kalimera, kyrios Alex*," a rich, husky voice intoned. "You want I call the boatyard and tell them you'll be late?"

Struggling up from sleep, Zoe found herself staring at a short, broad woman of about sixty or so, who was wearing a print housedress and apron and holding a tray of coffee and orange juice. The woman, whom she guessed must be Angelika, was obviously as startled as she. Zoe realized suddenly how they must look, curled together with their bare shoulders and tousled hair just visible above the blankets, not to mention the outline of his hand where it had closed over her breast in sleep.

Grumbling beside her, Alex stirred.

"*Parakalo, kyrios*," the housekeeper blurted, rattling the juice glass against the coffee cup as she set the tray down on his dresser. "I not realize...anyone else is here...."

"It's okay, Angelika." His voice was calm and reassuring as it reverberated close to Zoe's ear. His arms tightened around her. "But...as you can see...I have a guest. We'll be needing breakfast for two this morning."

Her eyes still wide, Angelika nodded. "I fix," she muttered, hastily withdrawing from the room.

As the door shut behind her, Zoe hid her face against the pillow. "What must she think of us?" she groaned. "You can't really expect me to go out there and face her?"

He laughed with a rich, contented sound and nipped at her earlobe. "Of course I can. She's going to get used to seeing you around here, if I have my way."

Regretfully she shook her head. "To catch us like that, in bed together.... She's older, and probably very conservative. You don't do this to her often, I hope?"

His flash of smile held only a trace of irony. "What do you think, sweetheart? You saw her face."

Alex was in the shower by the time she got on the phone. Alicia Morrow, Jim Haverhill's secretary and a rather staid woman, answered his private number. She had decided to be brief and she was thankful that the secretary couldn't see her, sitting cross-legged on Alex's bed with his robe falling open at the neck.

"Alicia, it's Zoe," she said in her most business-like manner. "I'm visiting friends out of town and I've been detained. I should be in by late this afternoon."

"Where are you?"

Merciful heaven, couldn't she have any secrets? "Tarpon Springs," she admitted, making a face.

"Hold on a minute." There was a muffled conversation at the other end of the line and then the secretary came on again. "Jim's here and he wants to talk to you," she said.

Already ambivalent about what she'd done, Zoe was embarrassed in the extreme to be caught visiting the very place she'd told her boss she couldn't abide.

But the governor didn't rag her or ask any awkward questions when he picked up the phone. "Alicia tells me you're down in Tarpon Springs again," he said matter-of-factly. "I'd like you to do me a favor and stay over for a while. I've decided to announce my Senate candidacy with a fund-raiser at Innisbrook Resort in about two weeks. I need you to make arrangements. Also to recruit campaign coordinators for the six-county Tampa Bay area. Got a pencil?"

Alex was dressed in the jeans and sweater that she guessed was his regular working uniform by the time she had finished her conversation. "What's up?" he asked, lifting one brow at the look on her face.

She didn't reply. Whether she wanted it or not, she now had an excuse to remain in the highly charged situation she'd created. The tasks the governor had outlined for her would more than take up her time until the banquet date. They would also keep her in town for the Greek holiday of Epiphany and give her far more of a chance than she needed to fall so deeply in love with Alex that she could never hope to pull away.

"It looks as if I won't be going back today, after all," she told him finally, explaining quietly about her assignment. "I won't be staying here," she added when he tried to take her into his arms. "Not with Angelika coming in to do up the sheets. We can still see each other. But it will cause less gossip if I rent a place."

The manager at Innisbrook suggested a furnished villa on the resort property when she drove the three or four miles over from Alex's house to see him. Transferring her luggage to it during the afternoon, she tried to convince herself that she could spend the requisite time in Tarpon Springs and not run into her grandmother—or make a commitment to Alex that she couldn't keep.

It'll be healthy for me to get this place out of my system once and for all, she thought as she sat at the little desk in her furnished condominium, twisting political arms over the telephone. She decided to deal with it like a grown woman, and walk away whole. But in truth, she could think with concentration of only one order of business. Despite the anguish her mother had suffered as a modern American woman trying to live the old-country Greek life-style, she herself was perilously on the verge of falling into a similar trap. So, she shrugged as she gave up and dialed the boat-yard number to let Alex know where she was staying. What's life without risk? He's a man in a million. And after the way it was with us, I can hardly be expected to walk away from him.

Still, she wouldn't sleep with him that night. Insisting she needed time and distance, she agreed to see him for dinner, but refused to give him anything more than a good-night kiss. It hadn't escaped her notice that people in the restaurant where they'd eaten had recognized him and commented with interest on their presence as a couple there. She declined, also, to spend any time at his house, claiming that Angelika reminded her of her grandmother and adding that she didn't care to read disapproval in those flat brown eyes.

"It's hardly disapproval you'd see, *krysi mou*," Alex argued as he lingered on her villa doorstep. "Oh, it's true that she asked me about you. To be specific, she wanted to know when we were getting married. You see, she wants me to settle down as much as my parents do, and she hopes it's serious between us. She isn't used to finding girls in my bed."

He had reported on the housekeeper's curiosity in a half-humorous, almost ironic vein, and Zoe didn't comment. Personally, it was the only way *she* could deal with the idea of marriage. Just the same, it was hard to ignore either the strong pull of him or the memories they had already made together. As he stood there, so tall and confident and curiously unhurried, it was as if he had all the time he needed to snare her at his disposal.

Relenting a little before sending him on his way, she promised to cook supper for him the next night at her villa. In her heart, she knew it would probably lead to bed. Yet that's what I want, she acknowledged later, looking at her own naked body and half-shuttered eyes in the mirror as she got ready for bed. I can't stay away from him—not for long.

The following afternoon Zoe went uptown to order the floral decorations for the governor's banquet. She decided to grasp her fear of the *Yaya* by the throat and shop in the small Greek grocery store where she'd gone on so many errands as a child.

Call it an experiment, she rationalized as she parked on the narrow street and entered the small, dim shop with its barrels of peppers, beautifully decorated tins of olive oil and sacks of dried chick peas. She paused beside a glass case filled with *kasseri* cheese, trays of olives and white blocks of feta swimming in whey. See if you turn to stone just for buying a few Greek groceries to please your man.

She was actually enjoying the selection of lettuce and lemons and olives, not to mention her chat with the friendly, dark-haired young woman behind the counter, when it happened. Two women, one of them old and both of them dressed in black, came in from the street. Zoe felt a prickle of something that might be apprehension as they paused at the meat counter to discuss the merits of the lamb roasts in rapid and theoretical Greek.

Her attention was diverted again and again to the older of the two, a woman about her grandmother's age who had the same heavy cheekbones and deep-set eyes. Though she was much smaller and older than the grandmother Zoe remembered, the woman's solid build and iron-gray hair were hauntingly familiar. So was her voice—one Zoe could swear she had heard a million times before, in direct conversation as a child and forever afterward in memory.

Light-headed and feeling a little sick, she felt rooted to the spot. No, *Yaya*, she pleaded, remembering with cruel clarity how she'd pulled at her grandmother's apron once, begging her to stop scolding her tearful mother over some pastry. I don't want to see you—not ever again.

Then the younger of the two women mentioned something about going next door to the bakery for bread. The older one nodded, casting a puzzled glance at Zoe before turning aside to finger some figs and tangerines in the window display.

A little sigh escaped her. She forced herself to relax, managing to draw breath more naturally as the storekeeper counted out her change. Ghosts again, she chided herself. You're not going to make another foolish scene or panic just because someone looks a little like *Yaya* or speaks the way she did. Old Greek women of her generation look much the same.

Thus she was all the more horrified and shaken when, seconds after she had turned her attention back to the sales clerk, an arthritic hand clutched possessively at her sleeve.

"Zoe...little one...it is really you?" the old woman croaked in Greek, her scent of cloves, woolen clothing and dusting powder so near that it was like inhaling a sudden whiff of the past. "I'm your grandmother, child. Why you don't come to see me all this time?"

The flood of Greek transfixed her as effectively as if she'd been nailed to the floor. All color drained from her face as she shrank back in anguish, unable to free herself completely of the old woman's touch.

"I...I don't know you..." she stammered in desperate English, her stricken gaze caught and held by an implacable brown one, filmy with age. Little rivulets of perspiration ran coldly down her sides beneath her clothing. "I'm sorry," she added in a smothered voice.

"But you must believe me. You've made . . . a terrible mistake . . ."

Yaya, who'd always known more English than she'd been willing to admit, clearly understood the fact that she was being rejected. "Is no mistake," she insisted in that throaty, terrible voice. "Don't you recognize me, Zoe? I know from your Uncle Fotis that you're here."

Clearly anxious to help, the store clerk stepped forward to translate. "She says that she's your grandmother," the young woman explained. "She mentions the name of someone called Fotis, whom she says is your uncle. Is there anything you wish me to tell her?"

Wrenching from *Yaya*'s grasp, Zoe stared at the clerk for a moment without comprehending. "Tell her she's mistaken!" she cried, forgetting her package and bolting for the door.

Tears she wouldn't let go were stinging her eyelids as she stumbled outside on the broken pavement. Too upset to watch her balance, she tripped and fell, skinning the heel of her hand and gashing her knee on a rough piece of concrete.

She didn't pause to assess the damage to her limbs or her clothing. I have to get away from here, she thought in panic, leaping to her feet and stripping her little import's gears as she pulled out into traffic. This time, though, she didn't entertain any thoughts of leaving town. With a pain like a big fist clenching in her stomach and her knee bleeding through the hole in her nylon, she headed straight for the only comfort she knew, the Kalandris boatyard and Alex, the way a hurt or frightened hurt child might run for home.

He was in the prototype shop when she found him. His pleasure at seeing her so unexpectedly dissolved into a frown as his eyes fastened on the dirt and blood on her knee, the torn stocking.

"What happened?" he demanded, striding forward to take her by the shoulders.

"Oh, Alex . . . just hold me."

Strong and safe, his arms came around her. With relief she burrowed against him, her tears finally free to fall. Bitterly they soaked through his sweater as she clutched him, unwilling in that moment that she should ever let him go.

He was the first to pull back a little. "Tell me what happened," he insisted, wincing as he bent down to examine her injury. "Have you been in an accident?"

Mutely she shook her head.

"What, then?"

Standing there, Zoe tried to absorb some of the deep comfort of him into the place where she hurt the most. "Something that only wounds the heart," she whispered.

His frown deepened. "This didn't involve your grandmother, did it, by any chance?"

"Yes." The single word came out of her like a sigh.

His honey-colored eyes darkened, and she thought he had the sudden look of a man who has lost one round in a very important battle. "Will you be all right to walk?" he asked after a moment, putting a protective arm back around her shoulders. "I have a first-aid kit in my office."

Seven

Feeling about ten years old but *cared* for, for the first time in years, Zoe perched on the edge of Alex's desk. Soap and water, then iodine stung as he cleaned her knee and bandaged it. Trying not to grimace too much, she recounted the sound and scent and feel of *Yaya*'s sudden, terrorizing demands, her own clumsy denial and flight. Not fully understanding her reasons, she wanted passionately for him to share that ragged gamut of emotion.

But while he seemed sympathetic and asked a few terse questions, he didn't comment very much. At last he reached up to wipe a smudge of mascara from her cheek.

"More battle scars," he said gently. "Do you think you might have spoken a few words to her at least?"

It was hardly the reaction she'd expected. She felt hurt and betrayed, and then bone weary. Biting her lip, she tried to ascribe his lack of empathy to the cultural differences between their two worlds. But she knew she was only making excuses because she loved him so much.

"You don't understand...."

"Maybe not." Alex's tawny eyes, usually so transparent, had gone opaque and almost expressionless. "I can't help but wonder, though, if some kind of truce could be called. Families are still families, and I'll give odds she cares for you very much. Knowing our old Greek women as I do, I'm certain the two of you once shared some happy moments."

To Zoe his implication was clear. Though Yaya Spritos might have felt hostility toward her daughter-in-law, her feelings about her son's small child would have been a far different matter. Greek grandmothers spoiled and fussed over the second generation of their own blood.

Sliding down from his desk and stuffing her torn panty hose into his wastebasket, Zoe summarily refused to consider what he was suggesting. But she had to admit, as she drove back to her villa while he followed in his Mercedes, that his observations had given her a troubling new slant on things.

Is it really possible, she wondered, tentatively reaching back into an era she had largely blotted from awareness. Did I ever sit on her knee and listen to stories from the old country with a child's unerring instinct for adult approval and love?

Shuttered and unfrequented like the old sponge market, Zoe's recollections of those years were stubbornly inaccessible to her conscious mind. It doesn't matter, anyway, she decided, falling into the familiar pattern of blame and anger that surfaced whenever

Yaya was in her thoughts. After what she did to Mom, I don't want her long-lost affection.

That evening, she and Alex were quiet together. They ate at a small out-of-the-way restaurant in Crystal Beach and then returned to her villa to watch an old Humphrey Bogart movie on television. It was almost a foregone conclusion that he would spend the night.

Yet she was surprised and touched to the quick that he expected only to hold her. Any need for time and distance erased by what had happened that afternoon, Zoe tangled her soft limbs with his hard, bronzed ones between the sheets. "Don't you want me, Alex?" she whispered, stroking and touching him so that his need sprang up, ready against the palm of her hand. "Don't you know how much I want you?"

As he slept beside her afterward, his beautiful body satiated with loving her, she realized something there'd only been time to guess at before. Her own eyes were heavy with sleep as she lay awake for a moment or two considering it. Funny, she thought. Something I never dreamed could happen to me is happening, and there's a part of me already too besotted to feel afraid.

The truth, if she wanted to face it, was as bluntly apparent as the presence of Alex Kalandris in her bed. When she'd first known him, a chance encounter with someone who'd only resembled her grandmother had sent her fleeing any possibility of involvement. Now, when the dreaded thing itself had actually happened, he was the refuge she sought. Because of him, she had no qualms about staying on to conclude the governor's business, despite the chance that the afternoon's trauma would be repeated. She would go uptown in the morning, as planned, to discuss the final draft of the sponge-exchange bill with his father, and keep her other appointments, albeit with a wary eye.

It's as if there have been two of me, she thought as she snuggled against him, ever since we made love in his big bed. One woman bears a grudge and wouldn't settle in this town on a bet. The other wants to spend her life making love to him.

When they met at the offices of Kalandris Enterprises, Alex's father invited her to attend the upcoming Epiphany church service with his family and dine afterward at his home.

"As you probably remember, it's a time of great celebration," Stavros told her. "We have hopes that Adonis will retrieve the cross, just as Alex did some years ago. You're family—the cousin of our Theo's Nick—and we'd like to have you with us. Besides—" he gave her a sidelong grin "—you'd be doing us a favor. If we want to see anything of Alex . . ."

Zoe smiled back, a little embarrassed. It wasn't hard to guess that Stavros had a lively imagination, and she knew not one scrap of gossip would escape his ears. I wonder how he feels about his son making love to me, she thought. Do I fit his criteria for what Alex called a "suitable woman"? Or does he consider this a temporary attachment to be tolerated for political reasons, one that will eventually run its course?

Whatever the case, she couldn't fault the older man for his tact, any more than she could blame him for wanting to see Alex happily married, with a family of his own. She'd appreciated his shrewd and humorous brand of masculinity from the first, and she knew that their liking was mutual. He would genuinely want her to say yes to his invitation.

She had reasons of her own to accept. For starters, it would please Alex if she became better acquainted with his family. And it would solve yet another problem, she realized. She'd been nurturing misgivings over a request from the Greek Orthodox archbishop that she attend the same church ceremonies as the governor's representative. If she arrived with the Kalandris family, she wouldn't have to sit alone in the cathedral with strangers.

"I'd be happy to come, Mr. Kalandris," she said belatedly, the telltale dimple flashing alongside her mouth as she mused how like his father Alex was in some ways. "I'm not sure what my powers of persuasion are with your son, but I'll do my best to turn him up for you."

It was not to be her only invitation from the Kalandris family that day. Cristina, Alex's mother, unexpectedly phoned in midevening. "Since you'll be with us for the holiday, I thought you might like to take part in some of the baking the day before," she proposed. "It's women's work, but it can be really pleasant, with all the dough and sweetmeats and honey and everyone's hands involved in it together."

A warm little feeling crept into Zoe's chest even as she cautioned herself that being intimate with them was the first step toward capitulation. Well, so far, I'm safe, she thought with some irony. Alex hasn't said or done anything to indicate that this is anything more than a temporary affair.

"I'd love to help out . . . if you think I wouldn't be in the way," she answered, throwing him a look across the room.

"You arranged it," she told him in mock accusation a minute later, putting down the phone as he came

over to take her in his arms. "Now it's not just a Greek
lover I'm involved with, it's a whole Greek family."

Shrugging, he inserted his hands under her robe.
"On the contrary, I didn't arrange anything," he said
with something of Stavros's calculating gleam. "I've
told my mother very little about you, if you want the
truth. But she's nobody's fool and she knows me well.
She's probably guessed that I'm in love with you."

His words echoed with force that night through the
fabric of their lovemaking. All the more powerful because they hadn't been spoken in the heat of lust, they
seemed to unlock within her a deep well of vulnerability and trust. From it, she gave and gave to him,
rubbing her soles on his muscled calves and clutching
at his buttocks to drag him more completely into her
body. *I want you to take from me until I have nothing
left to give,* she insisted silently as his movements carried her upward in an ever-mounting crescendo. *I want
to be the Parnassan nymph of the waterfall to your
Apollo—a willing receptacle for all your passion and
rapture.*

She was still mulling over what he'd said in a somewhat more sober light when she arrived the next day
at the Kalandris mansion for the holdiay baking. *I'm
in love with you,* he'd told her, quite calmly and matter-of-factly, as if he hadn't wanted her to mistake his
meaning. *How I longed to confess the truth just then,*
she admitted to herself as she rang the bell. *To tell him
that I feel the same way. But I'm too much of a coward to face the consequences.*

Again it was Alex's sister, Theo—more pregnant
looking than ever—who greeted her at the door.
"Come in, we're all expecting you," she said, a welcoming, if somewhat speculative, look on her face.

"Sophie, Adonis's girlfriend, is here, too, and she's anxious to meet you."

Feeling as if she'd been assigned to a similar category where Alex was concerned, and wondering if she was being interviewed for a more permanent position, Zoe followed Theo Nikolaides down the mansion's long central hallway. The kitchen was a big, high-ceilinged room with cream-colored wooden cabinets and Mediterranean tiles. It was dominated by a huge wooden worktable. Sun and breeze off the bayou across the road filtered in through a bank of double-hung windows.

Alex's mother, Cristina, was comfortably attired in a practical skirt and blouse covered by a voluminous apron. She was just uncovering a bowl of *phyllo* dough that Zoe guessed had been mixed earlier so that it would have time to "rest." Wearing her traditional black protected by a similar cover-up, Alex's grandmother was setting a young girl with light brown hair and wide, pretty eyes to the task of chopping almonds and walnuts.

Smiles warmed their trio of faces. "My dear, I'm so glad you could come," said Cristina, wiping floury hands. "You've met my husband's mother, Thalassa, whom we call *Yaya.* This is Sophie Demetrios, who has dated our Adonis for several years. Unfortunately Kon's wife, Stefania, couldn't get off from her accounting job today."

Liking them, but a little ill at ease, Zoe murmured a polite greeting.

The grandmother, who seemed friendly if somewhat reserved, replied in Greek. *"Pos is theh?"* she inquired, extending one thin, blue-veined hand.

Lightly Zoe took it and replied in kind, her use of the Greek causing the old woman's first tentative smile to widen. "So you are Alex's girl," she remarked, using the word *aga pimeni*, which Zoe knew had the connotation of "sweetheart." "I didn't know that when I met you before," the grandmother added.

To her chagrin, Zoe could feel a flush spreading over her neck and face. "We're good friends," she admitted.

"You speak a little of our language. Cristina tells me you're a Greek girl."

"Only on my father's side."

Without realizing it, Zoe had reverted to English, and Cristina translated rapidly, adding something to the effect that her mother-in-law should leave off questioning and give Sophie a chance to say hello. Then, the introductions over, she asked Zoe what task she would like to do.

"Theo and Sophie are making the filling and the syrup," she added. "Why don't you help *Yaya* and me roll out the dough?"

"It's been an awfully long time..."

"I'll show you. It isn't hard."

Handing Zoe an apron, Cristina got out the long, thin dowel that served as a rolling pin in many Greek kitchens. Yaya Kalandris spread flour over the surface of the table. Taking one of the balls of *phyllo* from a blue-and-white bowl, she patted it into a square. As Zoe watched, Cristina removed her enormous diamond rings and set them in a small dish on the counter. Her long-fingered hands as capable as those of her son, she rolled the dough up on the dowel and then unrolled it again, flattening it as she did so.

Then she repeated the process after dusting the dough with flour.

"Now you try," she told Zoe with an encouraging look.

A bit awkwardly, though she had the sudden, odd feeling of coming home to a comfortable ritual after many years' absence, Zoe placed her palms on the dowel, moving them from the center to the edges as the dough stretched and curled around it.

Smiling at her, Sophie hopped down from her stool and switched on some radio music. Over at the stove where she was cooking the syrup, Theo was humming as she worked.

When the dough was thin enough, Yaya Kalandris inserted her hands beneath it and began to stretch it gently, working her way toward the edges, until it was almost as thin as a leaf.

Cristina laughed, with little crinkles at the corners of dark golden eyes that were very like her son's. "She's much better at this than I am," she admitted, eliciting a half-hidden flash of humor and appreciation from her mother-in-law. "For one thing, she has much more experience. And I seldom have the opportunity to bake anymore."

Zoe glanced at her in surprise. "Do you work?"

Alex's mother shrugged. "Not a job for pay," she admitted, "though I think if I were your age today, I would want to take that route. I help my husband with the family business, as I have for years... in addition to working with community charities. I suppose that makes me seem a bit conservative to younger women like you and Sophie and my daughter-in-law. But I'm proud to say that Stavros respects my opinion and I have a voice in the decision making. I'm his Athene, his female wisdom he likes to say...."

The warmth in her voice as she spoke of her husband was unmistakable. Glancing at Alex's grandmother, Zoe saw approval and what might at one time have been the hard-won understanding of an older generation. As beautiful, intelligent and loving as Cristina is, she thought, it wouldn't surprise me if she once had to work very hard to earn Yaya Kalandris's respect.

Probably it had been difficult for the older woman to acknowledge that any girl could be good enough for her Stavros, though Cristina obviously was. Difficult for *any* old-fashioned mother of a much-loved son....

Unbidden, what Zoe considered to be her own grandmother's destructive love for Yannis Spritos came to mind. She pushed it firmly from her thoughts. I can't believe Alex's grandmother was ever like that, she thought. Or that Cristina would ever be.

Carefully Yaya Kalandris placed the first sheet of *phyllo* for baklava in the pan and brushed it with the melted butter Theo brought her. Feeling a bit easier and more expert with the dowel, Zoe rolled out a second one.

But when she tried to stretch it as Yaya Kalandris had done, it promptly tore. "Don't worry," Alex's grandmother soothed her in Greek at her elbow. "We mend it as we put it in the dish."

The baklava was finished and cut in diamond shapes to bake in the oven, and Zoe was chattering away in a comfortable mixture of English and Greek to Alex's female relatives as she patted strands of *kataifi* in place for a roll when suddenly Alex appeared.

Looking taller and even more masculine than usual in that roomful of women, he threw her an approving look as he kissed his grandmother and snatched up a taste of the walnut-cinnamon-brandy filling Sophie was making. Teasingly his brother's girl removed the bowl from his reach.

"Well," he said to his mother, ruffling Sophie's hair with evident fondness. "How's my best girl doing? Does she have any talent in the kitchen?"

A few weeks earlier—even a few days—and Zoe would have bristled at what she'd have considered an extremely sexist remark. She'd have disparaged it as typical of an arrogant and chauvinistic Greek male.

Now, with the insights she'd gained into Alex's character and values, as well as the perspectives Cristina had provided, she did nothing of the kind. With a warm feeling in the vicinity of her heart, she was able to savor his underlying tone of pride and affection.

She waited with trust for his mother to give her a good report, and she wasn't disappointed. As Cristina praised her dexterity with the dowel, the phone rang. "For you, Alex," said Theo, answering it.

"Business," he replied, making a face. "I'd better take it in the study...or else I'll be stealing from Sophie's divine concoction again."

Although left behind with the women of his family, Zoe felt a heightened sense of awareness just knowing he was in the house. In a little rush she realized how much she was enjoying what Cristina had modestly called "women's work," especially *because* it fitted the ancient culinary traditions of her childhood. To her own amazement, she had a resurgence of that oddly comforting feeling of having come home, there amid the bowls and pans and honey jars of an unfamiliar kitchen and a tribe of women who were essentially still strangers.

She didn't let herself picture too seriously what it would be like to be accepted by them as a relative, or have Alex coming home to *her* on holiday afternoons.

But she had softened and grown ready to yield to almost anything he might suggest when her tall Apollo returned from his business conversation and linked his arm through hers.

"Time to pay a little attention to me," he decreed, spiriting her out of the kitchen, sticky fingers and floury apron notwithstanding. "We have to keep your priorities straight, you know."

Sophie's music and the women's low talk followed them through the open windows as he led her out onto the porch and down across the grass to a tile-roofed summerhouse. Inside it was bare and dusty, with its built-in stone seats the only furnishings. Half-shuttered, the place looked seldom used, and the octagonal window walls let in only a dim pattern of light.

Alex pulled her up close to him in the shadows. His clean, sun-warmed scent filled her nostrils and she could feel the beautifully formed outline of his body against her, hard and sweet.

"How lovely you are, with that smudge of flour on your nose and your hair curling up tightly from the heat of the oven," he murmured, tilting up her chin so that she met his eyes.

"You're only saying that because you're a man and the way to your heart is through your stomach," she said, laughing. Leaning back just far enough to deny him a taste of her lips, she knew she'd give in to him in a moment. "I'd advise you to be careful, or you'll have flour all over your front," she added. "Everyone will know why you dragged me out here."

Alex grinned. He was looking inordinately pleased with her for teasing him. "They know, anyway," he said.

One hand tangling in the curls at her nape, he proceeded to go after what he wanted. A little sigh escaped her as he brought his mouth down on hers to explore it thoroughly with his tongue. I'm his, Zoe thought—far more than I've let him guess. Even when the fires of passion were banked, as she was certain they must be there on the grounds of his parents' home, she could feel the heat fusing the two of them. Each time they kissed, whether to join like thunder on his mythical mountainside, or just as part of a quiet evening under the same roof, their relationship deepened.

It was that depth, she knew, that Cristina had noted with an observant eye when he'd claimed her in the kitchen. Can it be that fate had really given me such a man, she marveled as he slipped his warm, loving hands under her blouse. If so, could I really be fool enough to give him up, even though so much stands between us?

Some of the barriers had fallen, she knew—the most recent of them that afternoon in Cristina Kalandris's sunny kitchen. Bitter memories and the specter of her grandmother remained, powerful deterrents indeed to what she was beginning to want more than anything in the world.

As these thoughts floated through her mind, Alex was exploring in his tender fashion. "No bra?" he queried, a satyrlike glint in his eyes.

His hands and mouth were sending warm little arrows of desire winging through her body, and Zoe gave herself up to their sweet aching. "I thought I'd make it easy for you today," she told him, suddenly wanting to fuel his longing.

"Don't let it be said that I refuse generosity."

Pulling her down with him on one of the stone benches, he slid her apron down from one shoulder and unbuttoned her blouse partway. A moment later, he was cupping one full breast in his hand so that he could take its hardened nipple into his mouth.

"More delicious even than Sophie's filling for the *kataifi*," he proclaimed, tasting her with his tongue. "I can't think of anything more pleasant . . . except being inside you . . . or watching you give this beautiful bounty to a child we had made together in love."

"Alex, please!" A little thrill of something akin to fear swept through her even while warmth spread, too, from the place inside her that was his. "We shouldn't talk about things like that."

"I don't see why not."

Outside there was the crunch of footsteps lightly crushing dry leaves among the grass. They could hear voices—those of Sophie and a young man Zoe didn't recognize. Quickly Alex covered her breast, shielding it from view.

"It's my brother Adonis and Sophie," he whispered. "Let's keep quiet. Maybe they'll go away."

With his other hand, he partially raised the shuttered cover to one of the summerhouse windows. Through the chink of light, Zoe caught sight of a darkly handsome young man, stunningly similar to Alex, though a little shorter, with a more boyish cast to his face. Looking up at him, Sophie was leaning her light brown head on his shoulder.

The next minute Adonis was glancing in their direction. His face wore a startled expression. Quickly he looked away, absorbing dark eyes very like his father's. Then, speaking to Sophie in a low tone, he turned and led her back up the path toward the house.

"I'd swear he saw us," Zoe breathed as Alex eased the shutter fall back into place. "Even though I know that's not possible."

"Mmm...." His mouth was at her breast again, sucking with gusto at its rosy bud. "As a matter of fact, he did see us, darling...or at least he saw me."

"But Alex..." She tried not to let the sensations he was causing distract her. "How could he have, if you didn't do something to attract his attention?" Then another thought struck her. "But if you *didn't*, why did they leave so suddenly, as if they'd changed their minds?"

"Must you ask so many questions, *krysi mou*?" Giving her a look of pure lust, Alex took off her apron altogether and undid the rest of her buttons so that both her breasts were exposed to the cool, late-afternoon air. Casually he began toying with the waistband of her slacks. "If you must know, I signaled him the place was occupied, that he'd have to bring Sophie back another day."

"You did *what*?" Incredulous, Zoe wouldn't let him undo her snaps. "I suppose you're telling me they came here for the same reason."

He shrugged. "They use it often. And I approve...they love each other and they're planning to be married when he graduates. Now tell me, my beautiful girl, why you're giving me such a problem with this waistband.''

A deep stab of longing knifed through her as the snaps gave way despite her resistance and her zipper parted beneath his fingers. "For God's sake, Alex," she objected weakly, "you're not planning to make love to me *here*?"

"If you won't talk to me about making babies, we have to find something else entertaining to do. Oh, I realize it would be more comfortable if we had some lounge cushions out here or even a pillow. But I'll give you my sweater for your knees."

If she lived to be a hundred, Zoe would never forget any detail of that afternoon. Lingering with her would be the moment when he at last drew her back to her feet and they stood there naked in the empty summerhouse, wrapped in each other's arms. Though she was aware that some member of his family might still catch them, she luxuriated in the feel of their two bodies, so spent and tingling and familiar now, each with the other. It occurred to her as she rested against the beating of his heart that their coming together had been all the sweeter for flouting discovery.

He's the kind of man I've always needed, she thought as they finally dressed and went back into the house. One whom I can trust with my most wanton and risk-taking self. Feeling thoroughly loved and disheveled and full of him, Zoe wondered if anyone could detect the telltale signs of lovemaking on her lips and the warm flush of her skin. For her part, she could read them easily in Alex's mussed hair and his deep, golden-eyed glimmer of satisfaction.

If his family guessed what they had been doing, they gave no sign. Only Adonis glanced at her once or twice in quiet speculation.

They treat me like one of them, she realized, almost as if they would welcome me into the family whenever Alex gave them the word. But she didn't dare to pursue that line of thinking too far, any more than she dared ponder his remarks in the summerhouse. Instead, as she'd been doing quite successfully for the past week, she held problems in abeyance. Relaxed and happy, she basked in the warmth of Alex's love and the company of his large, affectionate family. Such pleasures had been missing from her life for much too long.

Eight

Zoe felt her first tingle of apprehension the next morning as they arrived at Saint Nicholas Cathedral. It was a beautiful day, if somewhat cool for the divers. The light blue-and-white Greek flag was snapping smartly in the breeze beside Old Glory. People of all ages were thronging the steps.

Wide-eyed, she took in the red-cheeked children in their colorful costumes, the stocky old men in carefully pressed but outmoded suits who lounged against parked cars, conversing with the liberal use of their hands. As Alex linked his arm through hers, she inhaled the strong, musky perfume of a heavily made-up young woman with a thin gold ankle bracelet.

All around them, people were greeting and embracing with great warmth and a complete lack of self-consciousness. Even the young men in T-shirts and shorts who were Adonis's cohorts for the dive ex-

changed full hugs for luck, unashamed of the affectionate contact. As the Kalandris family paused to
speak to friends, Zoe watched a moppet in a starched
apron and colorful money belt run to her grandmother, to be promptly picked up and held. Near
them, a light-haired boy in the traditional stiff-skirted
tunic and velvet weskit twisted the tassel on his cap
while his mother and the girl's grandmother talked
together.

The pervasive love for children and sense of family
connectedness overwhelmed her almost as much as the
rapid and partly unintelligible din of Greek voices, the
crush of bodies and sharp, exhuberant outbursts of
laughter. I'm an outsider here, she thought with painful awareness, a stranger. And with the memory of
Mom's unhappiness in my heart, I'll always be.

"Zoe?" Alex said beside her ear. "What's wrong?"

"Nothing," she replied.

"Let's go in, then. The service is about to start."

Their pew was near the front of the cathedral, with
a good view of the sacristy and the altar with its gold
and ivory decorations. Sitting between Cristina and
Alex, with her thigh hard against Alex's, she resisted
leaning her head against his shoulder for support.

But she couldn't quell her slight dizziness or sense
of déjà vu as the cathedral filled up to the point that
those lucky enough to have seats were packed in
shoulder to shoulder. Her discomfort grew as the
archbishop and his entourage came out in opulent
white-and-gold robes. Compounding it as the service
commenced were the heat and the sober but powerful
Greek sermon, the sunlight glaring through Byzan-
tine stained glass, an overpowering aroma of incense.

Though her knowledge of Greek had come back more rapidly in recent weeks than she'd have thought possible, Zoe didn't really hear the archbishop's words about the significance of Epiphany for world peace, though she consciously understood most of their meaning.

Instead she was drowning in memories—lost in a vision of herself and the *Yaya* at a similar service many years before. Though her father and mother had been with them, it had been *Yaya* to whom she'd turned when the service droned on too long and the incense grew too oppressive for a child. And it had been *Yaya*'s broad and welcoming lap against which she'd laid her curly head.

Alex is right, she admitted, her distress mounting with the crescendo of an ancient hymn. *I did love and trust her once, though I'd completely forgotten it. That's what makes her behavior after my father's death so awful and too impossible to forgive.*

It struck her that, somewhere under the cathedral's overarching dome, her grandmother would be sitting, too. Perhaps *Yaya*'s brother, Fotis, the grandfather of Theo's Nick, who was also Zoe's own great-uncle, would be with her. More than likely though, Fotis would be outside with many of the other men his age, spinning nostalgic stories and talking politics. She would be alone.

Is she remembering those past scenes today, Zoe wondered with a sick feeling in the pit of her stomach. *Is she sorry now that she sent the rest of her family away?*

Suddenly the past seemed to rise up and choke her. Thick and suffocating, the incense invaded her nostrils. The archbishop's monotone as he prayed for the easing of international tensions seemed to recede until it was coming from a great distance. Gripping the back of the pew in front of her until her knuckles showed white, she felt as if she were going to faint.

"Zoe?" Alex asked, concern lining his face as he steadied her with one hand on her arm.

There was a rushing in her ears as she got to her feet. "I'm going to be sick," she whispered. "Please . . . I have to get out of here. I need some air."

Shutting out the surprised and worried faces of Cristina Kalandris and the other members of Alex's family, Zoe shook off the restraint of his hand and brushed past him, hurrying out of the pew. The world tilted alarmingly as she gained the aisle to meet a sea of staring faces. Seconds stretched into an eternity as she compulsively sought and found the filmy brown eyes she knew would be gazing with particular horror at her breach of etiquette.

Somehow she summoned her sense of self-preservation. Pushing down the aisle, she fought her way through the standing-room-only crowd of tourists and faithful in the vestibule to emerge once again into the brilliant sunlight.

Momentarily disoriented, she looked around her. A crowd almost as large as that inside the church was still milling about the steps. A television camera crew had parked across the street and she heard the crackle of a police radio. Almost fixedly, she stared at a costumed girl who was cradling a live dove between her palms. That's right, she thought with abstract clarity. The dove will be released during the part of the ceremony that takes place along the bayou.

Then Alex was beside her. *"Krysi mou,"* he said, putting the words like a question as one arm came around her.

"I can't go back in there," she whispered.

For a moment his eyes spoke eloquently of yet another battle lost. "You don't have to, sweetheart."

Continuing to shelter her in the curve of his arm, he led her down the steps. Beside the curb the crowd was thinner, and her breath eased back to its normal rhythm. His hands on her shoulders, Alex listened as she blamed her light-headedness on the incense and the density of the crowd, finally on her lack of breakfast.

"I told you it would be better to eat something," he reminded.

As if it were an echo from another lifetime, she remembered what her reply had been, "All I want for breakfast is you." God, how I love him, she thought. Why did I have to find him here?

Gently prodding her further, Alex elicited the full truth: memories of the *Yaya* and her parents had crowded close. "It'll be all right, Zoe, you'll see," he promised. "I'll stay here with you, and we'll watch the parade form up before we walk down to the bayou. Don't worry...nobody's going to say anything."

Incredibly he was right. Limiting herself to one concerned glance at Alex when finally she came out of the cathedral, Cristina seemed to read in his face the message that everything was under control. Leaning her head close to her husband's she appeared to pass the word along to him.

Her restraint only made Zoe regret her behavior more, particularly in view of her role as the governor's representative. She had very little to say as the drummers and brass players in their red uniforms lined up along Orange Street. Instead she just leaned against Alex's shoulder as the acolytes and altar boys began to take their place behind the standard bearers.

Finally the prelates who assisted in the service came out of the cathedral two by two in their brocaded vestments, preceding the archbishop himself. The girl with the dove took her position of honor, followed by a phalanx of gaily dressed children.

The procession and the band began to play a march with a distinctly Mediterranean air. People along the sidewalks began to move, many of them clutching symbolic sprigs of basil.

"C'mon," said Alex, taking her by the hand. "There'll be a mob over at the bayou already. I want us to get a good place."

The exercise, as she matched her stride to his long one, was something of a relief. They arrived at the little waterfront park across from the Dolphin Inn well ahead of the marchers. As Alex had predicted, people lined the bayou's steep, grassy banks under the live oaks and cedars, on all sides of the bunting-decked ceremonial platform. A second audience awaited the highlight of the festivities in boats. They were anchored as close as possible to the roped-off diving area with its semicircle of dinghies.

Because Alex's brother would be among the divers, everyone made way for them and they were able to secure an excellent vantage point. An old man in a dark suit who had removed his tie and stuffed it in his pocket clapped Alex on the shoulder. "Good fortune to young Adonis and to your family," he said with a tobacco-stained smile. "You know, Alex Kalandris, I can remember like it was yesterday when you came up holding the cross.''

Alex grinned, the lines of strain she had put there easing in his face. *"Epharisto, Kyrios Spyrides,"* he said. ''Nothing would please me more than to have Adonis be so lucky.''

Her fingers laced through his, Zoe tried to hold the trauma of the past hour at a remove. As the vanguard of the parade arrived, she contemplated the glimpse of her lover's past she'd been afforded through the old man's eyes. She watched with undisguised fascination when the squadron of divers suddenly appeared, to run down the dock and plunge into the icy water, evoking wild cheers and applause.

A moment later, when they climbed out soaked and shivering into the dinghies, she caught sight of Adonis. Sharing one of the tiny boats with two other divers, he balanced one bare foot carelessly on the rim as he threw one of his friends a laughing comment.

That's how Alex must have looked in the first flush of his manhood, she thought—still just a boy but with all the promise of the man he'd become. She knew that as he waited, keen eyed, for the diving contest to begin, he must be reliving that youthful triumph. If she was any judge of his character by now, it wasn't hard to guess how much his brother's success would mean to him.

The crowd hushed as the archbishop arrived at the platform. Once again he began to speak, drawing out the suspense and the tradition of the ceremony. She could discern only phrases, the ritual prayer of the *Kryrie Eleison*. For Zoe, it was different from what it had been inside the church. There, in the fresh breeze and dappled sunlight, the onlookers did not press and there was no smothering cloud of incense. Without realizing quite how it had come about, she found herself getting lost in the ceremony's ancient and expectant beauty.

Then the dove was tossed free to soar against the blue of the January sky. In their dinghies the divers tensed, and Alex squeezed her against his body in sharp anticipation. Savage concentration showed in every line of Adonis's legs and arms and shoulders. Somewhere in the crowd, Sophie would be digging her nails into her palms.

Slowly the archbishop raised his hand. In what seemed almost to be slow motion, the cross flashed out golden in a little arc. Screams of excitement went up from the crowd. The dark water of the bayou churned and boiled up as the divers shot in, flailing their elbows in wild pursuit.

Alex strained forward as heads bobbed under the water, came up, went down again. Seconds later, roars and cheers and whistles rang out as one hand was raised above the others, clutching the coveted prize.

"He has it!" Alex shouted.

She found herself hugging him for joy. Momentarily he lifted her off her feet. Then, catching her hand in an iron grip, he dragged her forward through the excited crush. A wave of quiet descended as Adonis climbed back onto the platform to receive the archbishop's blessing. Almost immediately, pandemonium was restored. A laughing, shouting throng raised Alex's young brother to their shoulders and then reluctantly put him down again. Tears streaming down her cheeks, Sophie ran to him and was kissed with fierce emotion, let go, then kissed again. The divers were hugging Adonis, too, and laughing as they parted their ranks so that his mother and father could do the same.

Finally it was Alex's turn. So alike despite the difference in their ages and height, he and Adonis held each other fast.

"I kept it in the family, big brother," Adonis said in Greek, pride and joy and something that might have been hero worship shining in his dark eyes.

"I know." Alex's golden ones, too, were glittering with emotion. "I love you, Adonis," he added simply. "I'm very proud of you today."

Dinner at the Kalandris mansion was very late. Adonis held court all afternoon, amid the exuberant comings and goings of relatives and friends. Watching him with Alex by his side, Zoe felt the brothers' closeness was a tangible thing; she knew what Alex's tribute to him that morning had meant. Along with Sophie's jubilant affection, it had equalled the golden cross in its significance.

For these brothers, their family is their lifeblood, she thought. The women they marry will have to be part of that.

They arrived later that evening at the famous Zorba's nightclub, to be escorted to a place of honor beside the dance floor. Zoe was thoughtful in her festive red silk dress. Alex seemed not to notice. When they arrived, the master of ceremonies interrupted the floor show. The sword dancer in her scanty Turkish costume stepped aside while Adonis and his party were introduced.

Drinks were brought and payment refused. The congratulations of the morning and afternoon began all over again. As the floor show resumed, Alex put one proprietary arm about her shoulders.

Following the sword dance there was a belly dancer, who made the obligatory tour of the room to have folding money stashed in her bra and low-cut trousers. She was followed by a slightly overweight torch singer in a black crepe dress.

Finally the floor was cleared for dancing. With uncontrived enthusiasm, one middle-aged man got up and another joined him in the *hasapiko*. Holding their arms out at shoulder height, they competed with keen good nature, while the crowd stomped and clapped its approval.

Both were handsome in a wiry, barrel-chested sort of way. The shorter of the two was the best dancer, and after a minute or two, his partner stood back to watch, applauding and then showering him with dollar bills that fluttered to the floor.

When they sat down, a man and a woman took their place to dance the *ballos*, or couples dance. Then somebody called for the Kalandris brothers and a chorus of voices took up the demand. Zoe caught Alex's swift grin of pleasure, Adonis's answering one, their parents' warm look of mutual pride.

"Come on, show us how it's done," insisted a young man, whom she recognized as one of the other divers. Taking a white handkerchief from his pocket, he extended it to Adonis as if he were inviting him to the *sousta*, or chain dance.

With a whispered comment to Sophie, Adonis got to his feet and passed the handkerchief to Alex. Kon leaned back in his chair. "I leave this to the experts," he remarked with his usual dryness.

Meanwhile Alex and Adonis were stepping out onto the floor. Each had left his jacket and tie behind. Their white shirts gleamed under the lights against deeply tanned skin. The bouzouki player, drummer, guitarist and violinist began to play, a half exuberant, half mournful and subtly wild rhythm richly infused with emotion. Somebody in the audience began to keep time with a tambourine.

Alex stretched out his arms. Adonis—five-foot-eleven, perhaps, to his six-foot-three—did the same. Matching their movements to the music with an ease that was as spontaneous as breathing, they began to dance several feet apart.

All over the closely packed room, women sighed and leaned forward as their husbands' and lovers' dark eyes gleamed in robust admiration.

For there was absolutely no doubt about it—these were two very special men. Both were beautifully made, with rugged and yet classically chiseled features, long, lean torsos, wide shoulders and narrow hips. Both knew how to use their bodies, with superb masculine confidence and a lack of inhibition that bespoke its own sexuality and power.

Adonis was the hero of the day, and the magic of his triumph clung to his every step. But it was Alex from whom Zoe, like many a woman in that room, couldn't take her eyes. In the prime of his manhood, he had the mature depth and force that could make a woman's heart catch in her throat. His flash of smile as he threw himself completely into the moment seemed to claim something deep inside her.

He doesn't shrink from admiration or from showing off his body, she realized. Nor does he indulge in false modesty about his ability and expertise. Of the two of them, he's the better dancer, yet he'll probably defer to his brother when the right moment comes. For him, this dance isn't a contest at all but a letting go for the sheer joy of it, a sharing of his particular essence with those he cares about most.

Watching him, Zoe knew all too well how the hard muscles of his torso felt in an intimate embrace. By now, she was well acquainted with the dominion of those arms and the vigorous thrust of those trim buttocks and thighs. In her most private places she had experienced the tug and caress of his generous mouth, and she had clutched with little cries at that thick dark hair and those shoulders in her most abandoned moments.

How I love him, she thought for the second time that day—most especially the profound life force that runs in him so strong and true. He was right when we met on the dock that evening. Greek men—at least *his* kind of Greek man—are liberated in the very best sense. It's the same spontaneity and openness he's giving to this dance that frees me to be so completely his when we make love.

As she watched, the music intensified. Suddenly Alex stepped back and yielded to his brother. Clapping out the rhythm with his hands, he gave Adonis his full attention and admiration.

At the proper time and with a proper disregard for its importance, he emptied his pockets to shower his brother with money. Adonis laughed, obviously pleased, and brushed aside a stray bill that caught in his hair.

The applause when they sat down, drenched with sweat and smiling from ear to ear, was deafening. Shyly Zoe reached up to kiss Alex on the cheek, her

first public gesture of affection. Surprised and clearly
delighted, he lifted her chin with one hand and kissed
her fully on the mouth.

"I have an announcement to make," Adonis was
saying.

Drawing apart, they turned in his direction.

Still on his feet, Alex's brother had a glass in his
hand. "On this day of great joy for me, my family and
friends, I want to thank everyone for their kindness,"
he said. "Also, with the permission of her parents and
at the beginning of my lucky year, I announce with
pride my engagement to marry. I propose a toast to
Sophie Demetrios, daughter of Helen and Paul Demetrios, my bride-to-be and the woman I love."

The words rang out, "To Sophie!"

Pulling his beaming fiancée up beside him, Adonis
held her hand aloft to show off the sparkle of a new
diamond ring. Stavros toasted next, while Cristina
hugged Sophie and welcomed her to the family. The
Demetrioses were at their table and Sophie's father
raised his glass in turn to praise Adonis and state his
approval of the match. More hugs and speeches and
congratulations followed.

As a fresh round of drinks arrived, everyone began
to talk happily of the wedding, which would be held
in June. Zoe listened with curiosity, carefully disguis-
ing her wistfulness as Sophie's gown was discussed and
the crowns of flowers linked with white ribbon that
would be placed on her and Adonis's heads and ex-
changed during the ceremony.

"Alex has consented to be the *koumbaros*, the best
man," Adonis asserted as he looked pointedly in their
direction. "I challenge him to follow my example and

get married himself one of these days. After all, the luck of the cross is not just for me, but for all of us.''

Taken aback, Zoe was thankful when Alex just laughed indulgently though his fingers tightened on her hand. A *sousta* was forming as a stocky older man with a weathered face came to sit beside Theo's Nick.

"That's your Great-Uncle Fotis," Theo whispered, leaning across the table. "I wasn't sure if you'd remember him."

Plainly her estrangement from her family was by this time common knowledge, though Theo had implied no criticism. Glancing at *Yaya*'s brother with trepidation, Zoe wasn't sure how to respond when he nodded and smiled in her direction. I hope I can avoid a direct confrontation, she thought, returning a faint smile and looking away.

She jumped up with an alacrity that made Alex smile when the handkerchief was passed to them and they were drawn into the chain of swaying dancers. "What am I supposed to do?" she asked in mock helplessness, the dimple flashing alongside her mouth.

He laughed. "Just keep time to the music. It's easy...one-two-three-kick...but you're free to put in your own variations."

To her surprise, her feet seemed to remember the way. Her hands held shoulder height in Alex's and another man's, she forgot Adonis's remark, her own reluctant envy of Sophie and even her great-uncle's lined and expectant face. Just letting herself go to the music and the moment, she seemed for the first time that day to be truly a part of things.

I love this, she thought, throwing Alex a delighted look as the line wound inside itself and they ducked beneath an archway of hands. Then she lost hold of him as the line parted to admit several newcomers. To her dismay, she found her hand gripped firmly by the square, sturdy fingers of her grandmother's brother. Packed into the crush of bodies, she couldn't pull away.

"Zoe, girl," he said, a gold tooth flashing as he smiled at her. "Don't you remember old Uncle Fotis?"

Distractedly she lost the beat and someone stepped on her foot, leaving a dusty mark. "It's...been a long time," she stammered.

"Too long." He was raising his voice over the laughter and the frantic music of the bouzouki, and she cringed that anyone else should hear. "Your grandmother..."

"Mr. Nikolaides, please..."

"Fotis," he insisted. "Uncle Fotis." He leaned closer to her ear. "You seem like a nice young lady," he said. "So tell me...when will you stop this grudge and visit Kalliopaea? Each day that goes by she waits for you."

Nine

Zoe decided to say nothing to Alex—either about Fotis Nikolaides's questions or her own promise to think over what he was suggesting, given merely to win his silence. It was a special day for the man she loved, and she didn't plan to do anything else stupid or childish to spoil it. Acting as if nothing had happened, she talked and laughed and danced in the line with an almost fervid intensity, then joined Alex in a romantic couples dance that drew them quite a few comments and stares.

Finally it was time for the fireworks display that would end the traditional Epiphany celebration. The Kalandris party walked the half block or so from Zorba's to the river together. As Alex and Zoe watched, their arms about each other, showy chrysanthemums and pinwheels of light burst against the night sky to gutter out in little firefalls of flame. From darkened side streets came the occasional crack and boom of a cherry bomb as teenage boys continued to observe the holiday. She could feel her lover's pleasant physical looseness from all their dancing as if it were her own.

I have a lot to think about and a lot to face, she realized, her thoughts straying back to her Great-Uncle Fotis for a moment. But for now I'm happy just being with Alex tonight.

Then she shivered at the cool night air on her bare arms and he settled his jacket around her shoulders.

"Come, *krysi mou*," he said, "it's getting cold out here. Anyway, I've been wanting to ask you something. Will you come home to stay with me tonight?"

She didn't answer him immediately, and he added, "Angelika's apartment is separated by a breezeway from the kitchen. I've told her not to disturb us in the morning until I call."

If that's what you said, then she knows the whole story already, Zoe thought. But the phrase "come home to stay with me" had caught fire in her imagination. What does it matter, she asked herself with a mental shrug. The whole town knows we're sleeping together and no one seems to care. Besides, unless I can find a way of solving the problems that separate us, we won't have each other forever.

"All right, darling," she said.

"Good." He gave her a little squeeze.

Bidding an affectionate good-night to his family, they walked to his car. To her surprise, when they unlocked his front door and entered his living room, she saw that someone had lit a fire. Several candelabra filled with hand-dipped candles flickered beside the hearth's *flokati* rug and soft woven pillows. There were also a bottle of champagne cooling in a silver bucket and a plate of honeyed sweets.

"I don't understand," Zoe began, turning to face him in the shifting light. "When did you have the time..."

A muscle quirked alongside his mouth. "If you must know, I arranged all this with my housekeeper early this morning. I called her from the club maybe forty-five minutes ago so she'd have time to light the fire and the candles. Don't give me that look...you and I have some unfinished business to transact in this setting, in case you don't remember."

But she'd only been feigning annoyance with him. Her dimple giving her away, Zoe stepped out of her shoes. The room felt warm after the cool air by the river, and Alex took his jacket from her shoulders to throw it over the couch. Funny, she thought as his hand went to her zipper. Each time we start this, I want you more. It's as if the place inside me that belongs to you can never get enough.

A moment later, the soft silk fabric of her dress was gleaming crimson about her ankles. She had worn no bra beneath it, and she stepped free to stand before him in just her ivory lace panties and the garter belt and sheer off-white stockings she'd bought at a local drugstore.

"Beautiful," he murmured, reaching out to stroke her breasts though his gaze slid lower past her slim waist and small, indented navel. "I suppose you realize underthings like those serve only one purpose...to give a man pleasure while he removes them."

Still she didn't answer. Instead her hands were at the front of his shirt, slowly unbuttoning it to reveal the dark hairy mat that covered his chest. Kissing it and his flat male nipples, she slipped the shirt completely from his shoulders.

"You're the beautiful one," she told him, running her gaze over his hard muscles and sun-bronzed skin. "No wonder all the women at Zorba's were coveting you with their eyes."

Something pleased and startled showed in his face at the forthright compliment. "I'm glad you think so, *Zoe, mou*," he said, one brow lifting at her a little. "You know how much I want to please you...."

I wish I had a photograph of us now, she thought as he pulled her into his arms to capture her lush softness against his chest. Just the way we're dressed—or partly undressed—how the light is, a little something of what we feel. I want to trap the whole erotic memory of it in my heart.

It took almost nothing, just a touch or a kiss, even a look from him, to excite her now. That the situation was mutual, he clearly demonstrated. Inserting his hand beneath ivory lace, he grasped her buttocks and pulled her tightly up against him as he invaded her mouth with his tongue.

How big and hard he is, she thought, half-wild with anticipation. Why doesn't he take off the rest of his things and let me touch him everywhere?

As if he could read her thoughts, Alex pulled back a little to hold her gently at arm's length. "I don't intend that we should hurry, sweet girl," he said. "I want time to stand still as we drink our champagne, taste the sweets Angelika left for us and make love to each other first with our eyes."

Though they'd each had quite a bit to drink, they had metabolized most of it with their dancing. She didn't object as he led her to sit down by the cushions. Her lips parting slightly, she watched as he removed his shoes, socks and trousers so that he was wearing only his undershorts.

Pouring champagne for both of them, he sat down beside her to clink his glass against hers. "To my brother Adonis and his timely suggestion," he proposed, his eyes raking suggestively over her body. "I should listen to him with more respect, don't you think, now that he's a man?"

Zoe prayed he would ascribe the flush that spread over her cheeks to the glow of the firelight. "You haven't bribed Angelika to put a potion in our drinks, have you?" she replied, ignoring his question to pose one of her own. "Because I'm already feeling much too strongly attracted to you."

"Taste and find out."

They sipped at their champagne, honey-colored eyes meeting violet-shadowed brown ones above the rims of their glasses. I'll let my question go for now, she had the sudden notion he had left unsaid. But I won't wait to ask it forever.

"Well?" he prompted.

"You bribed her. I want you even more than before."

Alex laughed, a deep, richly masculine sound gone faintly husky with desire. With a desultory gesture, he picked up the plate of rich desserts: *koulourakia*, baklava, *kourrabiedes* and tiny delicate pastries called "honey cups."

"Sweets to the indescribably delicious," he told her, filching one of the diamond-shaped baklava and licking some of the honey from it as he passed the plate to her.

Her eyes scarcely leaving his face, Zoe selected one of the sugar-powdered *kourrabiedes* before setting the plate aside. Deliberately resting her free hand on the hard shape of his knee, she began to taste the small, traditional wedding sweet as sensually as if she were tasting him.

Shaking his head at her, Alex wiped his mouth with a napkin. "Do you know how naturally sexy you are?" he asked. "Maybe I won't be able to keep my hands off you, after all."

A moment later he was casually unfastening first one set of garters and then the other. A shiver of pleasure raced over her skin as he smoothed down the sleek pale stockings, removing them and leaving a trail of kisses in their wake.

"And now for this charming contraption..."

Her mouth curving into a smile, Zoe helped him remove her garter belt, then wriggled free of her panties. "Don't you feel a bit overdressed in those shorts?" she asked, enjoying the warm firelight on her own nakedness. "Why not take them off, too? I want to make exquisite love to you."

With a narrow-eyed look, he complied. Always, even by the very gesture of recreating their first intimacy, Alex had taken the lead in their lovemaking. Now she wanted to assume it, at least temporarily—to ravish him as the women's eyes in the little Greek cabaret had ravished him, while staking her claim with every kiss and caress.

Restating her intentions in the direct and visceral language of touch, she straddled him to hug him with her knees. "Beautiful man," she whispered, proudly letting her breasts brush against his skin as she began her downward path of kisses.

Pure sensation was her object as she marked a loving trajectory along the hard planes and curves of his chest and thighs, moved on to his softer, more vulnerable stomach and midsection, the little hollow places beside his pelvic bones.

Ready for her, he groaned as she took him into her mouth. "Zoe...I'm at your mercy," he said, his voice rough and almost helpless as he cradled her curly head.

Reveling in her ability to arouse and tantalize, she set out to discover every nuance of his passion as she touched and licked and adored. He didn't try to muffle his groans and growls of pleasure. Beneath her, she could feel his magnificent body shudder and tense, give itself up to her ministrations.

You're a man who can be mastered, after all, my marauding Apollo, she exulted as finally she raised her head and moved upward so he could fill her. But did you realize that your shy nymph of the waterfall was really a lusty goddess in disguise?

Yet they were evenly matched and she knew it, lovers in the heroic sense if not the mythical one as he thrust upward to ignite her pleasure with his. Longing blazed up hot and sweet in a rush that almost took her breath away.

Later she wouldn't be able to say how long they moved together, herself mounting the crests like a ship's figurehead above his body. She wasn't even certain if their journey had proceeded with the swelling grandeur of a symphony or carried them up in a dizzying ascent of moments.

Instead she only knew that the climax was more profound than anything she'd ever experienced. The last walls of her separateness from him seemed permanently crushed and abandoned. It was as if she were being fused to his very essence, to become so much a part of him that he was like another self.

"Alex...oh, Alex...I love you so much," she gasped as she lay spent against the pounding of his heart.

His face was buried against the heat of her shoulder. "Can you realize how much I love *you*, darling girl?"

Afterward, as they settled down to sleep in his big bed, she reflected that she'd half expected him to elaborate on his toast. With a part of herself, she'd even hoped he'd pose the question she wanted so desperately to hear but couldn't really listen to or answer just yet.

Maybe I'm imagining it, she thought; maybe this is just another affair to him, something he doesn't anticipate will last.

But she knew better than that, even by the way he held her in sleep. Though her experience with men hadn't been very extensive, she was woman enough to read the signs. They all pointed to one thing: Alex wanted to make a home and have children with her. He wanted to draw her permanently within the circle of his love.

I want it, too, she thought—so much that it's like an ache lying aga...st my heart.

First the consequences of accepting what he might offer had to be reckoned with. Without question, there would be the sacrifice of her job with the governor and a move to Tarpon Springs. To do what? Open a gift shop or a candy store? Just be his wife, live the traditional role her mother had chafed against?

No, she reminded herself, you could go to law school, as he told you. Stetson's within easy driving distance, or you could commute to Gainesville and be home on the weekends.

Her original objections to the small Greek town where he lived and to his large Greek family had been largely answered. Time spent with Alex and the Kalandrises had radically altered her viewpoint. By no stretch of the imagination would Cristina ever take on the role Yaya Spritos had played in her daughter-in-law's life. Nor was the wily but warm-natured Stavros a disapproving and uncommunicative old man.

I've come to love them, she realized, almost as if they're the family I missed out on having so long ago. Gentle Theo and pretty, laughing Sophie, Adonis who's like a young Alex. I'm fond of them all, even Kon, with his dry, self-deprecating manner, and Yaya Kalandris, so observant and really friendly in her reserved fashion. If I left I'd miss all of them very much.

Even the town with its rough brick streets, tiny ethnic shops and dockside panoply of tourists had become a kind of home to her again. She had come to be fascinated with its rich fabric, where the strands of her past, present and possibly her future were woven in a secret design.

In reality, there was just one reason, one deep and abiding concern that she'd failed to lay to rest. Kalliopaea Spritos in her somber, threadbare widow's weeds still barred the way to Zoe's happiness. You have to deal with her, she admonished herself, find a way of laying that antipathy to rest, or give up everything you want.

In the morning, she couldn't raise the cup of confrontation to her lips. A week remained before the banquet at which Jim Haverhill would announce his Senate candidacy, and in Tallahassee, the special session of the legislature had convened to predictions in the press that it would readjourn quickly without having tackled much in the way of peripheral business.

I have enough to worry about at the moment without facing up to *Yaya*, she decided, rationalizing her procrastination in her mind. I swear I'll settle things once and for all when the banquet is over.

Getting on the phone, she spoke to Earl Mabry, the governor's legislative aide, only to learn that the bill providing purchase funds for the old sponge market had been tacitly labeled low priority.

"Do something, can't you?" she urged, foreseeing the kind of emotional fracas that would break out if her efforts failed and Stavros proceeded with his conversion project.

She could almost picture Mabry's shrug as his answer came over the wire. "To paraphrase an old saying—you can lead a bunch of legislators to water but you can't make 'em drink," he said. "If you want the truth, Zoe, I think this bill has a far better chance in the April session."

She knew that would be too late. Extracting a promise from Mabry to do what he could, she colored her update to Gus Andriotis with a subtle warning, then broached the facts with Stavros that afternoon in his office.

"Our agreement was for this month, not April," he reminded her, his brown eyes going flinty hard. "Alex explained it to you before…each day that we wait, the price tag of construction goes up dramatically. And there's an opportunity cost to reckon with. We lose the money we would have made if the conversion had been completed on schedule."

"I know how frustrating all this must seem," she agreed as her lover's father paced his plush, paneled office. "Working with elected officials always introduces an element of uncertainty."

"There's no uncertainty as far as I'm concerned." Stavros swung about to face her, combativeness evident in every line of his burly, muscular body. "I've told you before and I'll tell you again . . . if they fail to pass that bill, I'll have my wrecking equipment on the property within an hour. I don't plan to be delayed in this any further."

Sitting where she'd been the morning he'd introduced her to Alex, not realizing they'd already met, Zoe didn't answer him. What a shame something can't be done to satisfy both sides, she thought.

Watching her, Stavros allowed his harsh expression to soften. "Don't imagine that I blame you, my dear," he soothed. "You've done what you could. I know that."

He had halted beside her chair, and impulsively she reached out to take one square, powerful hand in hers. "I just hope it won't end in an impasse, Mr. Kalandris," she said.

Stavros nodded his leonine head. Then, in one of the abrupt mood shifts she knew him to be fully capable of, he gestured at a bookshelf lined with pictures of his grandchildren—Kon's and Stefania's two girls and the three-year-old boy belonging to Nick and Theo who would soon have a younger sister or brother.

"This project of the sponge exchange is important, I know that, but it isn't the issue of a lifetime," he told

her. "For me, as you've probably guessed, the para-
mount thing is family. Someday Alex will take my
place...both as the chief executive of Kalandris Enterprises and—so to speak—as the head of our clan.

"He's more than capable of the task...a compas-
sionate, intelligent and beautifully made man...the
kind of son any father would be proud to call his own.
He pleases me in everything, except for one overrid-
ing concern."

"I suppose you're going to tell me what that is."

Stavros shrugged, giving her a faintly ironic smile.
"Why shouldn't I? You're in love with him. No,
no...don't bother to put a casual front on things. It's
written all over your face. And because he loves you,
too, my feelings involve you, as well. Call it an older
man's greed for immortality, if you wish. But I want
to see him married...happily settled, with a family of
his own."

Resting one hand on her shoulder, Alex's father
nodded again at the row of family photographs.
"Cristina and I would be very pleased to have you for
our daughter-in-law," he said bluntly. "Don't be embarrassed. I wanted you to know...and to realize that
there's room in this grandfather's office for another
photo or two one of these days."

Hugging Stavros's approval to her like balm for the
wounds of childhood, Zoe completed her political
dinner arrangements. The day before the banquet,
Tim Bartram, the governor's public-relations coordi-
nator, came down to help. As they stood in the huge
banquet hall at Innisbrook resort, testing the public-
address system and checking out last-minute details,

she caught him observing her with a quizzical expression.

"You've changed," he noted in answer to a query on her part. "*Softened*, become more womanly somehow. What's going on, anyway? Have you fallen in love?"

Zoe rode over early on the night of the banquet with Tim to help supervise the setup and introduce the political coordinators she'd recruited for the governor's campaign to local newspaper and television reporters. Though Alex was to join her later as her guest for the evening, he'd warned her he'd be a little late.

To her chagrin, she ran into her ex-husband, Blaine Walker, even before locating Jim Haverhill.

"Well, Zoe!" he exclaimed, catching hold of her hands in the midst of the cocktail-party crowd. Pointedly he looked her up and down in her minimal white crocheted cotton top with its strategically located palm-tree appliqués and matching long, arrow-straight linen skirt. "I must say you look as if the single life agrees with you."

Annoyed at his warm tone, she gave him a stiff hello and withdrew her hands. "I suppose you came down on the plane with Jim," she said, pointedly ignoring his too-personal remarks. "Do you know where his is? The press is here. Tim and I really do need to find him."

Blaine grinned, his striking blond good looks a matter of total indifference to her now. "I expect he's back in the private suite, getting ready to make a grand entrance," he said. "Now about that sexy new look of yours and how you acquired it."

"Excuse me..." The high-pitched, almost quavery voice belonged to an elderly woman in a flower-print dress. "Aren't you state legislator Walker?" she asked. "I'm Hazel Coe, chairman of the Bryant Gardens Political Club."

Calling down blessings on the woman's neatly coiffed head, Zoe ducked away in the crowd. She didn't catch sight of Blaine again until the guests for the hundred-dollar-a-plate dinner were filing into the banquet hall and taking their seats. Stepping out of a little knot of politicos near the stage, he managed to catch hold of her arm. A moment later Alex walked in the door.

"Excuse me," she said coldly. "But my date for the evening has arrived."

"You don't say." Casting an appraising glance in Alex's direction, he gave a nasty, almost condescending chuckle. She caught the strong aroma of bourbon on his breath.

"So that's the Greek boyfriend I've been hearing about," he said. "Passable, I guess...if you like the type. What does he do for a living, anyway—dive for sponges? Or run a restaurant?"

Furious, Zoe brought the spike heel of her shoe down on Blaine's instep. His grip slackened as he smothered a pained little yelp of surprise.

"As a matter of fact, Alex is an attorney who runs his own boat-building company," she told him icily. "But it wouldn't matter to me what he did. He's man enough to make *ten* of you."

"Who was that?" Alex asked with a frown moments later as she took his arm.

His frown only deepened when she informed him of Blaine's identity. For the first time, she saw real anger and what might be jealousy in his amber eyes as the banquet and speech-making progressed. It didn't help matters any that her ex-husband kept glancing in their direction.

For her, the only bright spot in the evening was her opportunity to introduce Alex to Jim Haverhill. Without a doubt, the governor's approval was warm and unstinting.

"I'm very happy to meet someone who can make our Zoe bloom this way," Jim said, not pulling any punches. "You may be pleased to learn that I'm giving her a few mandatory days off following this event, for good behavior."

As she'd expected, Alex had taken to Jim Haverhill, too. But his look of annoyance at Blaine's attention to them didn't lessen. As soon as it was decently possible to do so, he pressed her to make her excuses and depart.

Like some kind of nemesis, Blaine turned up in the lobby as they were going out the door. "I'll phone you when you get back to Tallahassee, Zoe," he called after them, causing Alex's mouth to harden in a firm, uncompromising line. "It's high time we reminisced about the good old days."

Ten

Alex was silent in the car, his foot heavy on the gas pedal as they sped the short distance over Innisbrook's winding road to her rented villa. The Mercedes' big tires squealed to a halt beside it, an audible expression of his anger.

"Why are we stopping here?" Zoe ventured softly. "I thought we were going to sleep at your place tonight."

"Yours is closer." With a brusque little gesture he cut the engine. "We have some things to settle tonight."

They got out of the car. His hand was firm, almost impatient on her arm as she got out her key and fumbled with the lock.

"Alex," she began, opening the door and switching on a soft lamp, "I'm sorry if you thought—"

"Don't talk."

Reaching for her purse and keys, he tossed them down on the entryway table. Then, still holding fast to her arm, he led her through the small, impersonally furnished living room into her bedroom. With narrowed eyes, he jerked back the bedcovers so that they trailed over onto the floor.

"Take off your skirt," he said in a voice that brooked no resistance, as he shrugged off his dinner jacket and unfastened his belt.

Wide-eyed, she did as he requested.

"Your hose and panties, too." Rapidly he was stripping off his trousers.

Seconds later, they stood facing each other, naked below the waist. Ready for her, he grasped her by the hips. "Lie down, *Zoe, mou*," he demanded, more urgency than tenderness in his beautiful voice.

There would be no sweet initiation this time, she realized, no languorous playing at love. But it's not as if he's forcing me, she reasoned as she lay back against the sheets. I love him too much ever to deny him now. And I want him—even if it has to be this way.

She didn't have long to wait. He soon covered her and pushed in between her legs, his lust and readiness moistening the way. Lovingly she wrapped her knees and arms around him. But there was no gentleness in him, just a harsh uncompromising need for her that conquered everything in its path. His beloved face a passionate mask, he thrust deeply into her body, over and over again, as if by claiming her with the maximum ferocity he could erase all memory of Blaine Walker and her marriage to him.

Completely attuned to him now, she responded even to such furious lovemaking. Quivering with what he was making her feel, she arched to meet the full force of his invasion.

Their peak came in what seemed only moments, a shattering, violent paroxysm that jerked them up and then dropped them back against the mattress, heated and gasping for breath. Without a word, he rolled off her and they lay side by side, not quite touching.

The silence between them was absolute. Slowly then her fingers curled into his.

"Forgive me." Close beside her ear, Alex's voice was ragged with contrition.

"Hush, *andras mou*. You don't have to ask my pardon."

"Do I need to say it? I was wrong...I shouldn't have taken you that way...without making the time to show you my love."

Turning toward him, Zoe caressed the hard muscles of his arm and shoulder. "Maybe our coming together *was* a little fierce tonight," she admitted. "But it was good, too...knowing we can be that way for each other. You were right, Alex, in assuming that I'm yours to take."

He didn't answer, and guessing what he felt, she added, "I know you'd never force me, darling."

"Thank God I can agree with that...."

Smoothing back a stray curl from her forehead, he kissed her eyelids. "I can't bear to think of Blaine Walker ever having you," he said, his voice still gruff with emotion. "That's not an excuse, just a reason. It wasn't your fault, the way he kept undressing you with his eyes.

"I suppose now that you realize the truth—that I have my father's temper along with some of his good qualities—you'll say to yourself, 'What a typical

Greek he is . . . all passion and no sense, the kind of man my mother warned me about.'"

Loving him, she uttered a crude, one-word epithet.

A muscle quirked alongside his mouth. "Maybe," he conceded. "But I'll tell you one thing . . . I don't apologize for my unwillingness to share you with anyone."

"I don't want anyone but you," she answered.

He didn't seem to hear. Abruptly, as if there were a good deal of tension in him still, he got up and retrieved his trousers, patted about in their pockets for a cigarette. Watching him, Zoe realized that he smoked only rarely, usually when there was something on his mind. It's more than just Blaine and the way he was behaving, she intuited. I felt that tonight the minute Alex walked into the room.

Then she noticed the incongruous fact that they were still partly dressed, and sat up to pull her crocheted top over her head. Lying back against the rumpled sheets, she held out her arms. "Take off your shirt," she said. "Lie back down with me so we can go to sleep."

He gave her a swift look. "Sure you want me to stay?"

"I *love* you, Alex Kalandris . . . in case you're foolish enough to doubt it."

Mashing out the cigarette, he did as she suggested. A moment later he was beside her, putting his arms around her and slinging one long leg over her body.

"That's better," she said, insinuating herself against him.

Another small silence rested between them. "Probably what I regret most is spoiling our evening," he told her at last. "I wanted it to be perfect. There's something I wanted very much to ask."

So she'd been right to think something was on his mind. A half sick, half excited feeling knotted up inside her. "But you don't plan to ask it now?" she heard herself prodding him.

"Maybe the time isn't right."

Absently she stroked the fine hairs on his buttocks and thigh. I'm not ready for what he had considered saying to me, she thought. But I want very much to hear it, because I love him so much.

There was a part of her that yearned, childlike, for him to take all decision making out of her hands, compel her the way he'd compelled her with his body—no matter what problems there'd be left to face. Somehow we could make it right if we were together, she thought. *Couldn't we?*

"Oh, hell..." Alex drew her closer in his arms. "I might as well go ahead, even if the timing is bad. Now that your assignment here is finished, I don't want you to go. I'm afraid of losing you, when I've waited all my adult life to find you. I'm asking you to marry me, Zoe...pleading with you, demanding it, trying to convince you in any way I can that we should spend the rest of our days together."

His words like an echo between them, he continued to hold her. Zoe felt as if her heart would burst from wanting him and from all the love she felt, the urge she'd had almost from the beginning to give him joy. But, try as she would, whenever she pictured the kind of life they could have together, she saw only her grandmother's implacable face.

"Aren't you going to answer me," he prodded, a little catch in his voice. "Even if the answer is no?"

"Oh, Alex . . . if only it could be as you say."

"And you think it can't?" Plainly he didn't believe it.

Miserable she hid her head against his shoulder. "I just don't know."

He waited, hoping, she guessed, for the kind of explanation he deserved. "You've told me more than once that you love me," he reminded.

"Oh, I *do* . . . so much that it carries me away."

"Then what's the trouble, *krysi mou*? Why can't we be together?"

"Haven't you always known . . . and understood that you were taking a big chance loving me?"

He was silent a moment. "Yaya Spritos," he said.

She nodded. "Whenever I try to imagine us happy, the past gets in the way. You know I've put off facing her, though I've promised myself I would do it as soon as my assignment here was complete. Now that time has come, and I'm still not certain I can manage it. If I can't, what kind of a life could I have with you here? I'd always be thinking of her, expecting to run into her without warning, at the cathedral, the grocery shop. . . ."

"Ah, Zoe . . ." The empathy in his voice was clear, despite his obvious frustration. "You have to face it, sweetheart," he said gently. "I'll try not to push you, though I want to . . . with all my heart. Remember what the governor said—you have a few days off for good behavior. Use them to our advantage. Work out the problem of your grandmother so that Adonis's wedding needn't be the only one in my family's fortunate year."

In the morning a storm was blowing up. Great, ragged thunderclouds scudded in from the Gulf, blackening the sky and turning the pines an electric green by contrast. Shrugging off the weather and insisting he didn't want any breakfast, Alex went home to change for a day at the boatyard.

Alone in her rented villa Zoe faced her thoughts, and felt as if a dull little ache had settled around her heart.

I wish we'd stayed at Alex's house last night, she said to herself, so I'd be there this morning among his things—even if Angelika was a silent presence just beyond my solitude. Maybe it would be easier to surmount my fears and tackle what he's suggesting.

At the moment, though, doing that didn't seem easy at all. On impulse she got out her mother's faded photograph album, which she'd stuck in the side pocket of her suitcase, and slowly turned the pages. By now she realized that the Tarpon Springs her mother had known, with all the problems it had posed for an independent-minded woman, was largely an artifact of memory. Only *Yaya* remained, older certainly, but no so very changed from her pictures even today.

It's true what I told Alex last night, Zoe fretted, coming to the view of her parents on the front porch of *Yaya*'s house again. Each time I even think of facing her, something chokes up in my throat. I feel as if I'm paralyzed, yet at the same time angry enough to shake her.

With a sigh, she closed the album and rested one hand on it in her lap. Though by now it was late morning, the interior of her villa was dark—almost dark enough to turn on a lamp. Big, squally raindrops were beginning to strike the sliding-glass doors to her patio and she could see occasional bolts of lightning forking off beyond the trees.

To Zoe, the building storm was beautiful—wild, tempestuous and oddly satisfying, just as her and Alex's most recent lovemaking had been. Without a doubt, the dark weather matched her mood, and anyway, she wasn't afraid of lightning or thunder any more than she feared heights, fast cars or talking to irascible but important strangers.

Only *Yaya* makes a coward of me, she thought— even though she's an old woman who can't possibly do me harm.

Just then the phone rang. It was Alex. "It's storming like fury here," he said. "Are you all right, Zoe? Do you want me to take the day off and just come home to you?"

Without thinking, he'd spoken of the rented villa as "home" simply because she was there, and the effect wasn't lost on her. She managed to laugh a little, despite her mood. "Just because of a storm?" she asked.

For a moment, there was static on the line. "Not really," he admitted. "More because of last night and the kind of thing that's probably going through your mind today."

It would have been easy to accept his offer. But his presence the night before hadn't solved anything, and she believed that confronting *Yaya* was something she had to manage on her own. "I'll be fine," she told him. "You suggested I take this time to think about things, and that's what I'm trying to do."

Though he didn't seem completely satisfied, Alex didn't argue. "I'll see you about five-thirty, then, all right?" he asked. "We'll go out for dinner or something, if you want."

Putting down the phone, Zoe stared at the rain. It was coming down now in sheets, hardly creating an opportune moment to take action. Yet a small voice inside her was demanding she do just that. If you won't face *Yaya* for your own sake, do it for Alex's, it insisted. Loving him when you can pretend there's no tomorrow is easy. Put your courage where your heart is and drive your demons away.

A moment later she was on her feet, rummaging in the closet for the rain slicker that she'd borrowed while aboard his boat. Lacking an umbrella, she shoved the slicker's sou'wester hat down over her ears and grabbed up her keys.

The little import's headlights raked through heavy curtains of rain and its tires hydroplaned through the puddles as she drove out of the Innisbrook complex. Her heart in her throat, she headed for the older part of town, turning down Grand Boulevard and then for the first time onto Pericles Street.

There was very little traffic, probably because of the weather. She didn't even recognize the house at first, though she'd been looking at pictures of it less than an hour before. Its sloping porch and corrugated tin roof were the same. But it looked infinitely shabbier and smaller somehow than the house she remembered. At some time in the past following her departure with her mother, someone had painted it a nondescript shade of tan, erasing the white walls and blue door of memory. Only one very rusty metal chair stood beside the concrete urns, mute testimony to the solitary life of its occasional occupant.

Stopping the car, Zoe left the engine running. The wipers continued to beat back the rain. One hand on the door handle, she stared at the house and tried to imagine herself living here as a child. Yet though memories came flooding back, they seemed at a far remove, as if they were scenes from someone else's life.

Only her anger was real, blurring into a brooding sadness at the estrangement that had occurred in her family, when other families were privileged to share love and an unbroken safety net of memories, from generation to generation.

"Do it," said the voice inside herself. "Get out of the car and walk up on the porch, ring the bell. Lay your ghosts."

"I can't," another voice answered, the voice of nine-year-old Zoe who'd come down those steps for the last time on another rainy day, clutching her mother's hand and her small, cheap suitcase. That Zoe had hated the grandmother who stood behind them, and vowed never to forgive her—*even while she'd longed to turn and fling herself into the old woman's arms!*

I hated her because she didn't stop us, she realized in a stunning, painful insight, because she didn't call us back and beg us not to go. The truth was, I didn't want to leave her. I loved her, too, the way Alex said.

Slowly, like someone in a trance, she shut off the engine and got out of the car, forgetting about the headlights. But she couldn't seem to get any closer than the gutter, where she stood with her shoes half sunk in the rushing rainwater. Frozen in time, she saw a curtain move at one of the windows. A moment later the front door slowly opened.

From within the shadows of the doorway, the sturdy, black-clad figure of the *Yaya* faced her. *Zoe,* she seemed to be saying, though the torrents of rain swallowed up any sound. Just *Zoe*. No other greeting, no other word.

As if it were yesterday, Zoe saw again her mother's frail back, bent with the weight of their luggage, her wan, determined look, as if she knew what kind of financial and emotional struggle they would face. "No, *Yaya*, no!" she screamed silently, her eyes boring into the old woman's across the space of all those intervening years. "Not even for Alex. I can't ever come back to you."

Fumbling blindly with the door latch, she managed to get back into the car. At first the engine ground and wouldn't turn over. Her grandmother was still standing there, waiting, when finally it caught and she skidded and tore off down the wet, rough street. On Pinellas Avenue she slowed a little. *Oh, Yaya,* she thought, in a soundless cry straight from the heart. She didn't even notice that water was still dripping from the brim of her hat and running down her cheeks like tears.

She was back at the villa, throwing things into her suitcase and aching with the necessity of having to explain to Alex what had happened—when the phone rang again, jangling sharply through her consciousness. Briefly she considered not answering it.

Because it might be Alex, she picked up the receiver. To her complete surprise, the caller was Sophie, an agitated and extremely distraught Sophie, phoning from the gift shop where she worked on Dodacanese Boulevard.

"Come quick, Zoe!" Adonis's young fiancée spoke with a thin note of desperation. "I don't know what's happened, but the wrecking crew has moved into the sponge exchange! The old people are crying.''

Standing there holding the receiver, Zoe felt as if she'd been kicked in the stomach. Her personal anguish forgotten, she tried to calm Sophie and then dialed the governor's office in Tallahassee with shaking fingers.

"Jim's not here," the governor's secretary told her. "We tried to reach you, but there wasn't any answer. The legislature adjourned this morning without passing the sponge-exchange bill, despite our most vigorous protest. I understand it was on the midday news in the Tampa Bay area."

With all her connections in Tallahassee, there was nothing Zoe could do. Dialing again, she found that the phones at Kalandris Enterprises were busy—or off the hook. But it didn't matter. Stavros had told her his intentions in no uncertain terms, and she guessed it would be difficult, next to impossible to dissuade him now.

Maybe Alex...

Georgiou Pappadopoulos, Alex's assistant, answered at the boatyard. "I'm sorry, Mr. Kalandris went out a little while ago and didn't say where he was going," the foreman told her. "If you'll give me your number, Miss Walker, I'll have him return your call."

Swiftly Zoe ransacked her options. "Tell him to meet me down at the sponge exchange," she decided. "Say that his father has called in the wrecking equipment...and that I need him there with me, even if there's nothing he can do."

Slamming down the phone, she pulled on her wet slicker again and ran back out to the car. But she didn't really need the heavy garment, since by that time it was only slightly raining. She had little hope the faint drizzle would put a stop to wrecking opeations. Already the sun was burning a hole in the clouds.

I don't know why I feel I have to get involved in this, she thought as she drove at breakneck speed to the sponge docks. It's too late now, and anyway, I knew a week ago that this was probably in the offing.

In truth, despite her extended stay, she still didn't have an opinion on how the sponge market problem should be handled. In trying to resolve the conflict, she'd only been doing her job.

But she knew in her heart that affecting such benign disinterest at this point simply wouldn't wash. Though she wasn't sure which side in the controversy had the most defensible case she knew one thing for certain. Even if she'd probably be leaving it now, she cared about Tarpon Springs and its Greek community, about Sophie and the old people who were clinging to the past, more than she'd ever thought possible. At the same time, she wanted what was best for Stavros and the Kalandris family, wanted the progress they were proposing.

As she parked by the docks and ran alongside the moored yachts and shrimp boats toward the old market, she could see the little knot of grieving people. From within the market itself, came the screech and roar of heavy equipment, the dull thud and smack of the wrecking ball as it plowed into brick and stucco and wood.

A van with the insignia of a local TV station was parked at the curb and she spotted a cameraman and reporter, zeroing in on the crowd. The footage they were getting, she guessed, would be heartrending in the extreme.

Old people, grizzled men with weather-beaten faces who had once worked the boats when sponge fishing was in its heyday and broad, somberly dressed women who'd flirted shyly so long ago with the young divers they'd been, were pressing close to the iron gate Alex had unlocked for her nearly two months earlier.

Their hands gripped the bars and there was the low, almost keening sound of futile protest as they watched the past they cherished crumble before their eyes. It was as Sophie had said on the phone: tears were streaming down their faces.

I can understand how the old men feel about this place, Alex had said to her that very first night, even while he'd spoken of the benefits of progress. What words had he used? *They're sad to see a way of life disappearing in which they've sunk their best manhood years.*

Helpless, Zoe clenched her hands into fists to keep from crying. Oh, Alex, she implored silently. Where are you? I need you so much.

She didn't realize for a moment that someone was clutching at her sleeve. Then she turned to meet Sophie's agonized brown eyes.

"Can't you *do* something?" Adonis's fiancée pleaded breathlessly. "It's killing them. I thought it wasn't supposed to happen this way."

Eleven

At first Zoe could find no words to answer her. Sharing the anguish she saw on Sophie's face, she threw her arms impulsively around the girl and hugged her close.

Then she asked, "Where's Adonis? Did you try to call him?"

Sophie nodded. "I don't know where he is this afternoon."

"I couldn't reach Alex, either."

For a moment she considered. They might be helpless, but her position on the governor's staff ought to carry some weight. "Maybe I don't have any right to meddle in this at all," she said finally, "but I feel responsible... as if I should try to stop it, at least until both sides can sit down and talk one last time."

Mutely Sophie nodded her agreement.

"Well, let's try, then. Maybe we could go around back and find the opening where they brought in the equipment."

"I know where it is...."

With Sophie as her guide, Zoe splashed through the puddled alley behind a small restaurant and gift shop and pushed open a loosely made construction gate.

"Hey...where do you think you're going?" one of the workmen called after them in heavily accented English.

"To see the person in charge," Zoe shot back. "Can you tell me who that is?"

Another member of the crew, slim and blond with a ponytail hanging out from beneath his hard hat, saw fit to answer her. "That's him...with the mustache and red bandanna, darlin'. But he ain't gonna talk to you. I'm sorry to say we don't allow pretty ladies in here."

"Thanks." With Sophie tagging after her, Zoe cut him short and picked her way through the hail of plaster and dust toward the man who was overseeing the wrecking operation.

"Please...you have to stop this!" she shouted at him over the din. "At least give us a chance to talk to Mr. Kalandris before it's too late. Those people..."

Beside her, Sophie shielded her face from all the flying fragments. Like Zoe, she stood her ground.

The Kalandris foreman regarded the pair of them with a mixture of annoyance and astonishment. "Who the hell are you?" he asked, motioning for the wrecking operation to continue. "Better still, how'd you get in here? And what makes you think I take orders from you?"

Zoe thrust out her jaw. Tears she hadn't released before were running down her cheeks, streaking the grime that had settled there. A little murmur went up from the crowd as a bulldozer that had been shoving the rubble aside backed up and they became visible from the street.

"I'm not ordering you, I'm *asking* you," she replied, keeping her tone as reasonable as she could while still making herself heard. "On behalf of Governor Jim Haverhill, whom I represent..."

"Sure you do. And I represent the president of the United States. Listen, lady...run along and take your friend here with you before I throw you out. This is a hard-hat area."

Zoe dug in her heels. "Not until you listen to what I have to say."

Glancing at the front gate, the foreman clearly had visions of the crowd surging in if he forced Zoe and Sophie out that way. With an exasperated sigh, he grabbed each of them by the arm and began to propel them none too gently back toward the alleyway.

"Hold on a minute."

To Zoe's acute relief, Alex had come striding up to them, tall and stern-looking in jeans, sweater and tan poplin jacket.

Uncertainly the foreman dropped her arm. "These two sneaked in the back way, Mr. Kalandris," he muttered a trifle defensively. "I'm just puttin' them out for their own good. I got my orders from your father—"

"They're with me." Firmly Alex gathered Zoe and Adonis's fiancée into the circle of his protection. "I'm calling a halt to this job immediately," he said, his dark brows drawn together in an emphatic line.

Behind them, the wrecking ball smashed yet another gaping hole in one of the stalls that had formerly housed the catch of a particular sponge-fishing crew until auction day. With her peripheral vision, Zoe caught sight of the TV camera's winking red light and knew they were being taped for public consumption.

"Immediately!" Alex repeated, a little muscle working beside his mouth. "Do you understand me?"

"Yes, sir!"

His creased face a study in conflicting emotions, the foreman waved the wrecking operation to a standstill. A cheer went up from the crowd as the TV camera focused on the wrecking ball, which now hung motionless, then swung back to catch a close-up of them.

"There's gonna be hell to pay for this," the foreman was complaining. "Mr. Kalandris said—"

"Tell your men to go home. I'll answer to my father."

Silently they waited until the wrecking crew had left the site. Though many of the onlookers who had crowded close to the iron grating began to lament the destruction afresh, others were celebrating. Zoe heard Alex's name mentioned several times.

He disclaimed any praise. "A cheap victory... and an all too temporary one, I'm afraid," he observed. "Gus Andriotis is going to be on our necks, and Charlie Rakis, the foreman, was right. There *will* be hell to pay with my father. You two might as well come along with me and catch the brunt of it, too."

The crowd was thinning out as they locked up and got into Alex's car for the short drive to his father's office.

"Thank God you arrived when you did," Zoe whispered, linking her arm through his as he started the engine. "He really was going to throw us out of there."

"Yes," echoed Sophie from the back seat. "Do you think you can stop it permanently, Alex? Or will they be back at it in the morning?"

Alex glanced at Adonis's fiancée in his rearview mirror. "Frankly, I don't know if it *should* be stopped," he told her. "I understand the old people's grief. But I think the development idea is basically a sound one. I'm only sorry my father didn't see fit to warn everyone what to expect this afternoon."

I agree with him, Zoe thought as they pulled into the gravel parking lot at Kalandris Enterprises. And yet I feel so involved now—as if I have to find some kind of solution that's satisfactory to both sides.

Stavros Kalandris was glowering as they walked into his book-lined office. "I just got one hell of a phone call from Charlie Rakis," he greeted them bluntly. "And I don't like what he had to say."

"Then neither of us is happy." Alex bit off the words in the same hard-edged tone. "Because I don't like the way you handled things this afternoon...no matter what your reasons."

For a moment the two men, so alike and yet so different, locked wills, and Zoe wondered if Alex would retreat into the proper respect due from a son in a traditional Greek family.

But he did not. Stavros's glance flickered over to her and Sophie again. "Forgive me, my dear young ladies," he said tersely. "But you don't need to listen to this."

Alex gave a little shrug that indicated only the slightest willingness to make things easier for his father. "Sophie needn't stay, if you don't think it's appropriate," he said, squeezing the girl's hand to let her know the remark wasn't personal, "but Zoe has a stake in this. It would have been simple courtesy on your part to inform her of your intentions, you know."

"Hell, the legislature didn't notify me they wanted to string me along for a couple more months. Anyway, I already did what you said...almost a week ago. She'll tell you."

Anxious to conciliate between them, Zoe nodded in affirmation.

Stubbornly Alex shook his head. "Not good enough. A week ago this issue wasn't settled yet...one way or the other. I don't suppose you told Gus Andriotis what you were about to do, either. And I didn't notice you down there at the docks this afternoon, *pateras mou*, taking the heat."

Zoe, who knew a little about Stavros now, saw that Alex's jab had hit the mark. "So? What if I wasn't?" he retorted angrily. "I gave Andriotis and that rabble of his plenty of opportunity to come up with an alternate plan. I'll be damned if I'm going to wait around any longer...or take any more phone calls telling me the son who should be supporting my position in this has countermanded my orders. In case you don't remember, I'm still president of this company and you run the boatyard. I won't tolerate this kind of interference from you."

Her hand on Alex's arm, Zoe could feel him struggling to restrain a deeply hurtful reply. Just then Stavros's secretary poked her head in the door. "Mr. Andriotis calling again, sir," she said apologetically. "He insists on talking to you."

"Tell him to go to hell," Stavros said.

Alex swore.

"No... wait." Zoe laid one hand on the secretary's arm, detaining her. "Listen, Mr. Kalandris," she said. "I'm as much or more to blame than Alex for stopping the wrecking operation this afternoon. But that doesn't mean either of us really opposes you on this project." She paused; incredibly she saw that she had his attention.

"Then why?" he asked, obviously interested in the notion that they were really on the same side. "You're a nice girl, Zoe. Why make so much trouble for me?"

Realizing her opportunity, Zoé chose her words with care. "Maybe you know that when I first came here, I didn't want any part of the Greek community," she admitted. "I didn't care then what happened to this project. Now I do...to the extent that I don't want the old people hurt. Please don't tell Mr. Andriotis off yet. Earlier this afternoon I couldn't reach Jim Haverhill. Let me call Tallahassee one more time and see if there's anything he can do."

Stavros looked at Alex, then back at her again. Slowly he nodded, waved her to the phone on his desk.

While she was dialing, Adonis and an older man she recognized as Stavros's brother, Tryfon, came into the room. Adonis put one arm around Sophie and wiped a smudge of dirt off her cheek. Meanwhile Stavros, Tryfon and Alex argued together in low, intense voices.

Jim Haverhill picked up his private phone on the third ring. He listened in silence as Zoe described what had happened in Tarpon Springs that afternoon from her own perspective. But when she asked him for options or encouragement he had none to give. "The situation has blown up in our faces," he advised, as coolly practical as ever. "The best thing you can do is disassociate yourself from it and come home."

Stavros was waiting when she put down the phone. "Alex has explained that you want everyone to talk again before demolition resumes," he said, apparently on better terms with his eldest son again. "I can't see what it's going to accomplish, but I'm willing to try it one more time because you say so. My secretary is asking Gus Andriotis to meet us here tomorrow at ten o'clock. You have until then to figure something out, Zoe. After that we're going ahead."

Alex was forced to fend off the press—both television and print this time—as they went back out to the car.

"It was telling him the truth about how you felt when you first came here that made the difference," he remarked quietly as they drove back to her villa so she could pick up a change of clothing. "Straightforwardness is something my father appreciates. That's why he didn't stay angry at me today."

"I'd never want to cause trouble between the two of you," she replied.

"You couldn't do that. Anyway, he's made it plain he wants you in the family...almost as much as I do."

Sunk up to her neck in political problems, Zoe let his comment slip away without an answer. At the villa she didn't demur when Alex followed her into the bedroom. Simultaneously they halted. There, forgotten in the wake of the day's events, her half-packed suitcases lay on the bed like an accusation.

For a moment Alex didn't say anything. "Were you getting your things together to move in with me?" he asked after a moment in a soft, perfectly controlled voice. "Or just planning to go away again without saying goodbye?"

Some of the cornered feeling she'd had when his father introduced them two months earlier returned, all the more vividly for the layer of memory. She felt guilty and ashamed for hurting him—and not a little afraid that he'd only take so much more of her childish fears.

"I wouldn't have gone this time without telling you," she whispered. "I started packing up this afternoon... after trying to confront my grandmother. I failed, Alex. Miserably. I parked across from her house and I was trying to get up the courage to go in, when she came to the door. One look at her and I fled...like all the demons of hell were after me."

Strong and tender, his arms came around her, even as something decisive glinted in his honey-colored eyes. "Don't think of it now, Zoe," he said, declining to make any recriminations. "Just come home with me and we'll talk about what can be done—if anything—with the sponge-market property. Leave the problem of your grandmother to me."

Adonis and Sophie were waiting for them in Alex's driveway. Alex turned on the evening news, and the four of them sat down to watch the program together. To Zoe, the poignant little scene featuring the construction foreman, the weeping crowd and their own unself-conscious and somehow alien faces seemed heightened into a drama of broader significance by the selectivity of camera angles and editing. To her relief, the reporting on the piece was factual and succinct. It's like a Euripidean tragedy, she thought as the brief cut faded to a commercial. Yet—fodder for the mill of current events—it would be forgotten a year from now except by the handful of old people who had been present at the gate.

She was quiet, almost pensive, as their guests talked and finished the pizza Adonis had brought, finally departing so that she and Alex were alone together.

"You hinted that a compromise would be ideal, the evening we met," she reminded as he switched off the TV, built a fire, then motioned her to come sit beside him. "But you said neither side would agree to it. Do you remember what kind of compromise it was?"

Frowning, Alex shook his head. "Nothing specific was ever worked out that I recall."

"Well, I've been wondering...the easternmost part of the exchange is still standing and most of the structural outline is in place even if some of the walls are gone. What if your father altered his plans a little, preserved a few of the old stalls as an exhibit of the town's cultural heritage? That way he would have his progress and the old people could have their history... in a much more accessible form than before."

Outside, it had started to rain again. Stretching out his long legs in front of the blaze, Alex gave her a thoughtful look. "You know," he speculated, "it just might work... *if* we can get my father and Gus Andriotis to listen to you. That won't be easy. You know from experience, don't you, how difficult Greeks can be?"

That night Zoe knew they wouldn't make love. While Alex dozed before the fire, she showered and put on a thin cotton nightdress. But when they went in to turn back the covers on his big bed, he asked her to sleep naked in his arms.

"I want to feel you, *krysi mou*, in my arms," he said, lightly crumpling the delicate batiste as he pushed it up over her body. "Even when we have things other than lovemaking on our minds. If I have my way...and I intend to have it...you'd better get used to that."

I want this man for always, she admitted, curling down in the deep comfort of his arms. Seduced by the warmth and scent and feel of him, she abandoned herself to fantasies of sitting in a third-year law-school classroom with their first child growing in her body, of arriving with Alex and two chubby toddlers at the Kalandris mansion sometime later to take part in holiday festivities.

If I know him, the fire between us would burn as swiftly out of control even if we had a family, she thought as his hard legs tangled with her smooth ones under the sheets. He'd still want to risk discovery by making love to me in the summerhouse, and invite me to half-naked picnics by the fire once the children were safely asleep.

In the morning Zoe dressed with care for the coming confrontation at Stavros Kalandris's office. Instead of a businesslike suit, she chose a soft ivory wool dress with long sleeves and covered buttons, the sort of thing she'd never in her life worn to a business meeting before.

"Good choice," said Alex, knotting his tie as he watched her brush her short, unruly curls to a bronze-gold sheen. "My father's just old-fashioned enough for the feminine approach to win you some points."

She cast him a sidelong glance. "What about his son?"

He shrugged, gave her a wicked grin she knew was intended to allay her nervousness. "I like you best in

your lovely satin skin," he said. "But, then, I
wouldn't care to have anyone else see you that way.
Nor would I be inclined to listen to any business deal-
ings you might propose."

We look like we're on our way to church or to a
justice-of-the-peace wedding, she thought as they got
into the car. I wish the daydreams I let myself spin last
night could be real.

Still, she didn't expect them to be, any more than
she expected Stavros and Gus Andriotis, Blaine's
probable opponent in the upcoming congressional
race, to compromise on her plan. Just the same, she
was determined to push for its acceptance to whatever
extent she could as they walked into the Kalandris
Enterprises boardroom.

Everyone else had arrived early. Tight-lipped and
angry-looking, Andriotis waited on one side of the
big, curving table with a delegation of his staunchest
supporters. Opposite them sat Kon, Tryfon and Stavros, saying nothing. Cristina, doubtlessly present as
moral support for her husband, was pouring coffee for
everyone. As if to emphasize his position of neutral-
ity and possibly of support for her, Adonis sat alone
at one end of the table.

Before either Zoe or Stavros could say anything,
Andriotis hit her with a barrage of questions. It wasn't
any secret that they were designed to castigate her, the
governor and the state for mismanagement of the situation, while implying that the Kalandris family, and
Stavros in particular, prized money above their common Greek heritage. Aware that much of the bluster
and invective was for political effect and that most of
their statements would probably be repeated to the

press if they failed to reach a compromise, Zoe bore it all with grace.

Stavros wasn't so inclined. "I want to hear what Miss Walker has to say," he interrupted, holding up one square, powerful hand for silence. "It was her idea that we meet today, not mine. I want to know if she has a worthwhile course of action to propose."

Summoning her best professional manner, Zoe outlined the plan she had described to Alex the night before, emphasizing both the opportunity for historical preservation and the commercial shot in the arm the new shopping plaza would bring.

"If I know you, Mr. Kalandris, the price of restoring several stalls as a tribute to Greek enterprise here would seem negligible in comparison with the benefits," she concluded. "Whereas *you* must realise, Mr. Andriotis...in its dilapidated state, the old market was hardly a tribute to anything. I'm sure you're both in favor of progress that doesn't trample on the past."

A massive silence greeted her words. Even if there's a chance they'll agree, neither of them wants to be the first to say so, Zoe realized. All I can hope is that someone—preferably someone other than Alex—will break the ice.

With a quick glance in her direction, Adonis seemed to read her thoughts. "I'm hardly the voice of authority here," he offered, "but the idea makes more sense than anything else I've heard. It will prove once and for all to this town, *pateras mou*, that we have everyone's interests at heart."

Stavros looked at Cristina. "I agree with Adonis... and Zoe," she said.

"Alex?"

"The same. Not for personal reasons, but because it's best."

Slowly Kon and Tryfon nodded, adding their unexpected support.

"Well?" said Stavros, still belligerent as he looked at Gus Andriotis across the table. "If I say yes to this, are you going to bargain for more?"

There was a long pause as Andriotis huddled with his supporters. During it, the phone rang and Alex answered it. "When?" he asked, his face breaking into a smile. "That's wonderful! Are they both all right? Mom will want to talk to you."

Moments later he was passing the receiver to Cristina. "Theo's had her baby!" he exulted, including everyone, even the Andriotis party, in the news. "It's another boy...and healthy, all strapping seven pounds ten ounces of him. She's fine. Both she and Nick are very happy."

The announcement seemed to put an entirely different complexion on things. A joyous expression on her face, Cristina was speaking softly to her son-in-law over the phone. Meanwhile Stavros was grinning from ear to ear.

Even Andriotis seemed to take the news as a personal stroke of good fortune. "Congratulations, you old bull," he said to Stavros in Greek. "That's one more grandchild than I've got."

"Epharisto, epharisto." Too pleased to contain himself, Stavros put his arms around Kon and Tryfon, hugged them close. "Now how about it, you old shark?" he shot across to Andriotis. "Are you planning to drive a hard bargain with a new grandfather?"

Still smiling, Andriotis switched back to English. "Hell, why should I?" he asked. "In essence, we're getting what we wanted."

"Then it's a deal!" Exuberantly, Stavros called for ouzo to drink a toast.

"At this hour of the morning?" Cristina protested with a smile, putting down the phone.

"Sure, why not?" Stavros drew her next into his bearlike embrace. "We've got a new grandson and, thanks to Zoe, old Gus and I are friends again. Kon, call the crew and tell them to get started immediately with their new instructions. Adonis, you go down and put up a sign. Let people know what we decided today."

To Zoe's amazement, all recrimination between the two factions seemed to have melted away. As if the hostility had never been, everyone was slapping everyone else on the back. Ouzo and congratulations were flowing. If only it could be this easy with *Yaya* and me, Zoe thought, gripped by a sudden, all-pervasive sadness. Then I could have the man I love and be a real part of all this celebrating today.

As usual, Alex seemed to know what was on her mind. Quietly he slipped an arm about her waist. "Hard to believe, isn't it?" he said, kissing her on the mouth. "But good Greeks don't bear grudges. And that reminds me...there's somebody we have to go and see today."

Twelve

No, Alex.'' Guessing his intent, Zoe struggled with him as overtly as she dared.

Neither her protests, nor the slightly raised eyebrows of everyone in the room availed. Impervious to all resistance, he escorted her forcibly out of the room. "It's time," he said, handing her into the Mercedes with calm authority. "Past time, in my opinion. In case you didn't realize it, I'm doing this for both of us."

Before she could think of getting out, or remember that her own car was still parked a few blocks away, near the sponge exchange, he had started the engine.

"I won't go in," she told him adamantly, keeping as much distance between them as possible.

"Yes, you will. And I'll be right there beside you."

"I have nothing to say to her."

He didn't reply. Fear, anger and all the old hurts that had plagued her for so long came welling up as they drove, powerfully enough that she considered asking him to stop the car so that she could part company with her breakfast.

Well, he can take me over to *Yaya*'s house, and even drag me up to the door, Zoe thought, compressing her lips. But he can't force me to speak to her, or "settle things" between us, the way he expects. If that were possible, I'd have done it a long time ago.

It seemed just moments later that he was parking across from the *Yaya*'s tan frame cottage—in exactly the same spot she'd stood the day before, letting the rainwater flow over her shoes.

Today, the rough brick street and patchy, sand-spur-choked lawn in front of her grandmother's house were dry. And she had nowhere to run to escape Alex's tender but firm insistence as he opened the door on the passenger side and took her hand.

"No," she said again, pulling back from him a little. "I *can't* do this . . . even if I wanted to."

"Yes, you can. Where's your pride, Zoe? Handle this like the grown woman your grandmother expects you to be."

Stung by his implied criticism, she got out of the car. "If I had any real pride, I wouldn't let you do this to me," she muttered.

"I'm doing it *with* you," he corrected, drawing her up the crumbling concrete walk. "There's a difference. I should have given you my support when you first needed it . . . several weeks ago."

Standing there with him on the little porch while he rang the bell, Zoe clung to Alex's hand as if to a lifeline. Shamelessly she bargained with fate that her grandmother wouldn't be at home. We'll have to leave, she fantasized. I'll be able to postpone any confrontation.

Then her hopes were dashed as slowly the door opened and the *Yaya* stood before them. For a moment Zoe and her grandmother stared at each other. Getting more than just a terrified glimpse this time, Zoe really looked and saw what she hadn't wanted to see in the store, or the cathedral, especially not through yesterday's curtain of rain. Though her fear had imparted to *Yaya* an imaginary agelessness and power, harsh reality was quite different. Her grandmother, more bent and frail than Zoe had thought possible, shifted her gaze to Alex, an almost pathetic question in her eyes.

"Kalispera, Kyria Spritos," he said in Greek, his tone conveying the utmost politeness and respect. "I have brought your granddaughter to visit you."

Nodding, the old woman stepped back a little. One arthritic and slightly shaky hand held open the screen. "Please come in," *Yaya* answered in her husky, well-remembered voice.

Like one in a dream, Zoe allowed Alex to lead her into a sparsely furnished parlor she only vaguely remembered. Awkwardly she sat beside him on a worn and lumpy couch while *Yaya* lowered herself painfully into a straight-backed chair. What if she *is* old now, and infirm, and doesn't really have anyone, she thought angrily. Does that excuse everything that happened? Alex wasn't there. He doesn't understand how it is.

Yet he'd reminded her good Greeks didn't carry a grudge. . . .

She stiffened as her grandmother began to speak again, breaking an uncomfortable silence. "I have wait long time to see you, Zoe," she said, using the English words haltingly, as if they came only with great effort to her mind. "You are a woman now...with my Yannis's eyes."

In the car, Zoe had determined angrily not to respond but simply to glare at the old woman in stony silence. Instead she found herself answering. "I'm told I look more like my mother," she retorted, deliberately rubbing salt into a wound.

To her surprise, *Yaya* agreed. "Yes, you have the same...how you say it...light skin and pretty hair," she answered. "Tell me, please...what is like, your life today...."

In response to a reassuring nudge from Alex, Zoe gave a brief, unwilling account of her job, her college degree and her place of residence, pointedly leaving out any mention of her former marriage and Blaine.

"My mother died several years ago," she added, becoming a little strident on the words. "She was sick for a long time. We didn't have any money, and there wasn't much I could do to help."

Listening intently, *Yaya* nodded. "I am sorry for that," she said with apparently genuine sympathy. "It is too bad things turn out this way. Please to excuse...I forget my *phyloxenia*, my hospitality. I get us some tea."

Alex's arm came around Zoe as the old woman shuffled off to the kitchen. "Why not go after her and offer to help?" he suggested in a low tone.

Stubbornly Zoe shook her head. "How can she say she's sorry, like that, as if it had nothing to do with her?" she countered in an outraged whisper.

He shrugged. "Maybe she sees your mother somewhat differently from the way you saw her . . . less as a
victim and more as someone who rejected her husband's way of life. I can't believe your grandmother
hated her the way you think. Isn't that a picture of
both your parents, there on the TV set?"

Stunned, Zoe acknowledged a framed black-and-
white photograph that had been taken at her own
baptism. I don't believe it, she thought. Surely she has
other pictures of her Yannis and doesn't have to tolerate the likeness of her unwanted daughter-in-law
after all these years.

A quick glance around confirmed her speculation,
leaving her more confused than before. Several other
photographs of her father, including one that had been
taken on his graduation from high school, were scattered around the old-fashioned room. With them were
quite a few snapshots of Zoe herself, carefully arranged by age and stopping short with a view of her
nine-year-old self on the steps of Saint Nicholas Cathedral.

Greek Easter, she thought. I can actually remember that occasion—and the night before, too, when we
attended the candlelight parade. That was just before
my father died. . . .

"I don't doubt for a minute that Yaya Spritos
wasn't always kind to your mother," Alex went on,
speaking softly to her though she refused to meet his
eyes. "Maybe sometimes she was even cruel. It's as I
told you the night we met. Our old people can be un-
believably clannish, and I don't excuse that. But
maybe your mother didn't give her much of a chance,
either. Maybe she hated having to live here, and let her
resentment show."

"No, *you're wrong*," Zoe whispered.

Even as she said it, memories flooded back, images of her mother balking at really learning the language, picking at her *kalamari* or *dolmathes*, only pretending to learn the intricate routine of pastry making.

I don't blame her if she didn't want those things to be the sum total of her existence, she thought. But she could have tried to fit in a little harder than she did....

It struck her with force that her grandmother, who was coming back into the room with a tray of iced tea and date confections, shared those unflattering memories of Zoe's mother, too. Maybe they were *both* wrong, and neither of them could help it, Zoe thought. Seeing *Yaya* again, just being in this house, is giving me back pieces of my past I haven't wanted to face.

Murmuring a polite, barely audible thank-you, she drank her tea in silence. When finally she put down her glass, the old woman leaned forward unexpectedly to put one blue-veined hand over hers. Longing to pull away from her, Zoe endured her touch.

"Your mother and I . . . we not get along so good," *Yaya* admitted, pain glittering in her hooded brown eyes. "Who is wrong, who is right . . . is no way to know that now. But I tell you this, I make big mistake the way I treat her after my Yannis dies. And I have plenty time to be sorry . . . twenty years, without the granddaughter I love. If you say is okay, I want now that we are friends."

Casting a desperate glance at Alex, Zoe suddenly found courage, comfort and a sense of direction is his faint, approving smile. I suspect he's right about my Mother, she thought with a lump in her throat—even if I don't want to believe it. But I won't love her any the less because of it. Maybe I could give some of the benefit of that understanding to *Yaya*, too.

Trembling a little, but feeling emotionally stronger than she had in years, she turned back to her grandmother. "After all this time, it won't be so easy, *Yaya*," she conceded hesitantly. "But I'm willing to give it a try."

"Is good." Briefly the old woman squeezed her hand.

They talked a few minutes longer, more easily now, though the situation was still awkward, about the nature of Zoe's assignment in Tarpon Springs and the happy outcome of the sponge-market problem. Buried in her welter of emotions, Zoe knew, was unmistakable pride in *Yaya*'s obvious awe of her accomplishments.

"So you go back to...to Tallahassee now?" her grandmother asked finally. "Not stay here, where people love you?"

Again Zoe shot a swift look at Alex. "I've been asking her the same thing, *kyria*," he said, amusement hovering at the corners of his mouth. "But she hasn't seen fit to answer me yet."

Clearly the *Yaya* understood his meaning. Zoe tried to hide her answering smile, though she did a fairly poor job of it. After all, things weren't on a completely even keel between her and her grandmother yet. And she hadn't quite forgiven Alex for riding roughshod over all her objections.

She didn't hesitate when he indicated that they should go. For a first time, the visit had been long enough, and there would be other times to come, now that the first barrier was past.

At the door she shook her grandmother's hand, promised to return. Somehow, though, a formal handshake didn't seem to be enough. Hesitating at the curb, she looked up at Alex, her brown eyes brimming with emotion.

"Go ahead, sweetheart," he encouraged. "I'll wait for you."

Released by his words, she ran back up the walk and took the old woman into her arms. She was only partly aware that her tears were spilling and that her grandmother was crying as well.

When at last they drew apart again, Zoe held tightly for a moment to the old woman's hands. "I've needed you, too, *Yaya*," she blurted, feeling as if she'd truly come home at last. "I can't tell you...how much I've needed you, too."

In the car Alex gathered her to him without a word. She didn't want to say anything, either, just to get in touch with her profound relief and the odd, light feeling of having a stone rolled away from her heart. Gratefully she let her hard-earned right to have Alex forever seep into her consciousness.

But her relief wasn't just for what the two of them could share. Some of it was for *Yaya*, regaining her lost history and the new role her grandmother would play in her life.

"Okay?" Alex said finally, kissing her lightly on the mouth.

She nodded. "I'm happy and sad and a little shaky, too. But I *am* okay, darling...thanks to you."

"Not to me. I only helped you look at what you were ready to see."

He was right, of course. As they pulled away from the curb, Zoe nestled against his shoulder. A part of her *had* been ready to give way, had longed to reclaim the Greek self that Alex's love and the friendship of his family had nourished after such a long, arid time. With after-the-fact clarity, she realized how much she'd wanted a reconciliation, even if it had to be bittersweet.

Absorbed in her thoughts, she didn't really watch to see which way they were heading. Thus she looked up with surprise as they pulled into the driveway of her villa.

Stopping the car, Alex held out his hand for her key. "Now that everything's settled, you'll have to finish packing," he said. "I'll be good enough to help."

Automatically she dug her keys out of her purse. Then, remembering how high-handed he'd been in taking charge of her life, she pretended not to understand.

"What do you mean, 'settled'?" she asked with exaggerated innocence. "Just where are you proposing we take my things?"

An answering glint in his eyes told her that if she wanted to tease him now that all serious objections were behind them, he would gladly play the game. "Don't you know you're coming home with me tonight?" he asked.

Zoe tilted her head to one side. "And just stay with you, now that my assignment is finished, I suppose."

"We won't be staying long. Now give me the key, Zoe. Before I explain, I intend making love to you."

Her telltale dimple flashing, she slipped the keyholder back into her purse. "I'm not sure I like being ordered about this way," she said thoughtfully. "Maybe I'm half Greek, but I'm a far cry from the old-country bride your parents once envisioned for you. I think we'd better get that straight.''

In response, one of his dark brows lifted a little; she thought she'd never seen such a loving look on his face. ''Well,'' he said with a little shrug, ''if you'd rather we did it in the car...''

A moment later she was thanking heaven for smoked-glass windows as he lowered the Mercedes' plush passenger seat to its reclining position. Like some determined god lusting after the nymph of his choice, he unbuttoned her white woolen bodice and slipped his fingers between her silky camisole and her skin.

''Tell me this isn't what you want,'' he murmured, lightly and sensuously tracing one delicate peak. ''If you can't, then you'd better confess the truth. You're irresistibly attracted to me and everything I stand for...even the old myths and traditions, the warm and volatile extended family that means....''

''Am I?'' Her voice came out husky and breathless.

He nodded. ''That's why you're going to marry me...as I've known you would since the night we met by Uncle Tryfon's boat.'' Lovingly he ran his other hand up her calf, stroking along her thigh with the tips of his fingers.

''But I don't want to live with the old ways—at least not exclusively—any more than my mother did.''

''Ah, Zoe, don't you know by now how it would be with me? How you'd be a free independent woman...*and* a cherished Greek wife? I swear it, darling, you'll have the best of both worlds.''

Turning serious, he pushed up her skirt to unfasten her stockings and slip them down her legs. Hot currents of anticipation knifed through her, making her ache with a sudden, implosive heat.

"Please," she begged. "Let's go inside. I can't have you out here... not the way I want."

In answer he tugged off her wispy, almost non-existent panties. Her hand slid with involuntary need to the front of his trousers. "I want *you*," she pleaded. "Deep inside me... most especially today."

"Then say it." With tender ruthlessness he sought and found the core of her desire, to coax it with consummate artistry. "Say you'll marry me, Zoe and let me love you all your days."

Rapacious and loving, he was kissing her neck and bare shoulder as his more intimate caress mounted a spiral of imperious pleasure. Ever more precariously, she was poised on the brink. Yet she needed more from him, far more at that moment—the complete union of their bodies that could truly nourish the soul.

Helplessly she had begun to arch against him. "Yes," she cried, not realizing in that moment she was shouting it. "Oh, yes... I'll marry you, Alex. Only *please*, darling... take me inside to bed."

Though his eyes had narrowed to passionate slits, she caught a tawny glimmer of triumph. "No need, *krysi mou*," he whispered. "You can have right here what pleases you best."

Afterward she would wonder how he managed it, with his long legs and extraordinary height—even though as automobiles went, the Mercedes was roomier than most.

In the heat of their longing, it seemed the most inevitable thing in the world. There was a rasp as his zipper parted, and then he was pushing between her legs, pressing her back against the seat's reclining angle with his weight.

Once again thankful for the dark windows that hid them, she raised her knees. She clutched him to her, eagerly opening her body and tilting forward to meet his thrust of entry.

For a moment he gripped her tightly, holding the two of them very still. Then he said in a gruff tone, "Forgive me, precious girl, but I don't think today I can make it last...."

Warmth was gathering in her like a tidal wave. "Go ahead," she urged, the words blunted against his mouth. "I need you badly, too, just taking and taking everything I have to give...."

He didn't require any further invitation. Fiercely he began to move, his rhythm catching her up in a wild and uncontrollable spiral of delight. When they reached the peak of their union, it seemed to rearrange the universe. Lifted out of control, she felt tears wetting her cheeks even as her soles and inner thighs tingled with discharged energy.

Crying out unrestrainedly in his own release, Alex sagged against her body. "My God, but I love you," he growled after a moment. "More than life, in case you didn't know it."

She smoothed his damp brow. "It's the way I love you."

Feeling complete and powerful and full of him, she didn't want the moment to pass. But they couldn't stay that way for long.

Deep within her a little tongue of amusement curled, and a giggle surfaced, communicated with something he was feeling, too. A moment later they were helpless again, this time with uproarious laughter, shaking until their sides hurt and fresh tears were streaming down her face.

"For God's sake, Alex, get off me," she pleaded, pushing affectionately at him while she tried to catch her breath. "Unless I can straighten up soon, I won't ever be able to walk again."

"*You* won't!" Still chuckling, he tried to move his long legs without much success. "I vote we call for help," he said. "Maybe someone in this complex has a giant can opener!"

Finally, after an intimate struggle, he had managed to extricate himself and they were sitting in their proper places. Zoe, who had partially done up the front of her dress, was smoothing down her skirt and stuffing her discarded stockings and panties in her purse as he lowered the windows for some air.

Her eyebrows went up a little as he rummaged for a cigarette. "Come clean, sweetheart," she said, patting her hair in place. "What's on your mind? And what did you mean before when you said we wouldn't be staying long?"

"Oh, that...." He slipped the unlit cigarette back in his case. "I wondered if you caught it."

Pausing to rub his shin where he had grazed it trying to get back behind the wheel, Alex took an envelope out of his pocket.

Zoe's eyes widened. "Airline tickets?" she asked. "*And my passport?* I don't understand."

"Carole sent the passport at my request, and the tickets are for our honeymoon. If you'll agree, we'll go to Clearwater tomorrow for blood tests. On Friday, my cousin John, who is a judge in Tampa, can marry us at the airport."

He was going a little too fast. Still, with her own plans for bearing his children and going to law school, she wasn't far behind him. "Where are we going?" she said.

"To Greece...if you don't object, *Zoe mou*. I want to share with you everything I found there alone—the sea like sapphires, glittering below rocky islets with their blinding white monasteries and villas, ruined temples and wildflowers on the mountainsides. We'll swim together in that sea, darling, and climb those meadows, looking for our mountain torrent. Make love every way there is to make it and settle all the questions of the universe as we sail from port to port."

So much love in his eyes that she was humbled before it, he took her by the shoulders. "We'll take our time, my beloved," he added. "I want to string the days together for you like diamonds, give you soft, endless nights full of love. You know, don't you, that the wedding night of Zeus and his bride lasted three hundred years? Ours will take at least that long."

"Oh, Alex." Overcome by the beauty of what he was suggesting, she slipped her arms around him. "I'm so happy...."

"So am I, *krysi mou*. Speaking of diamonds, the other day when you were trying to call me about the sponge exchange, I was at the jewelry shop, picking out this ring for you."

Taking possession of her hand, Alex slipped a beautiful diamond, set in platinum, on her finger. "With this ring, I thee wed," he told her. "As far as I'm concerned, the ceremony at the airport will be just a confirmation so that one day we won't embarrass our grandchildren. From this moment forward, I'm your husband in my heart."

Losing herself in his embrace, Zoe marveled at the kind of man he was and the unexpectedly generous fate that had made him hers. I'll really get to have him now, she thought, have him and love him always.

Still, something unsettled nagged at her, a certain unreasonable regret. "Sophie and Adonis's wedding in the cathedral," she whispered. "The crowns of flowers and the candles and all the relatives...both yours and mine. Maybe it isn't fair to them, even if *we* don't mind missing that. Maybe we should wait."

"Oh, no." Approval and something deeper, a frank and radiant happiness, gleamed in his honey-colored eyes. "I refuse to put off going away with you," he said. "But if you like, sweet Zoe, we'll have a second wedding when we return, for the sake of tradition and our families and the wedding pictures our children will see someday. But you'll have to pay the price for two weddings, darling...an additional three hundred years of love."

 Silhouette Desire

COMING NEXT MONTH

EYE OF THE TIGER—Diana Palmer
Eleanor had once loved Keegan—handsome, wealthy and to the manor born. The differences between them were great, and time hadn't changed them. But the passion was still there too.

DECEPTIONS—Annette Broadrick
Although Lisa and Drew were separated, the movie stars agreed to make a film together. Would on-camera sparks rekindle passionate flames off-camera as well?

HOT PROPERTIES—Suzanne Forster
Sunny and Gray were rival talk-show hosts, brought together in a ratings ploy. Their on-air chemistry sent the numbers soaring—but not as high as Sunny's heart!

LAST YEAR'S HUNK—Marie Nicole
Travis wanted to be known for his acting, not his biceps.
C. J. Parker could help him, but business and pleasure don't always mix . . . and she had more than business in mind.

PENNIES IN THE FOUNTAIN—Robin Elliott
Why was Megan James involved with big-time crook Frankie Bodeen? Detective Steel Danner had to know. He'd fallen in love at first sight, and he was determined to prove her innocence.

CHALLENGE THE FATES—Jo Ann Algermissen
Her child might be alive! Had Autumn and Luke been victims of a cruel lie—and could they pick up the pieces and right the wrongs of the past?

AVAILABLE THIS MONTH:

THE FIRE OF SPRING
Elizabeth Lowell

THE SANDCASTLE MAN
Nicole Monet

LOGICAL CHOICE
Amanda Lee

CONFESS TO APOLLO
Suzanne Carey

SPLIT IMAGES
Naomi Horton

UNFINISHED RHAPSODY
Gina Caimi

Take 4 Silhouette Intimate Moments novels FREE

Then preview 4 brand new Silhouette Intimate Moments® novels —delivered to your door every month—for 15 days as soon as they are published. When you decide to keep them, you pay just $2.25 each ($2.50 each, in Canada), *with no shipping, handling, or other charges of any kind!*

Silhouette Intimate Moments novels are not for everyone. They were created to give you a more detailed, more exciting reading experience, filled with romantic fantasy, intense sensuality, and stirring passion.

The first 4 Silhouette Intimate Moments novels are absolutely FREE and without obligation, yours to keep. You can cancel at any time.

You'll also receive a FREE subscription to the Silhouette Books Newsletter as long as you remain a member. Each issue is filled with news on upcoming titles, interviews with your favorite authors, even their favorite recipes.

To get your 4 FREE books, fill out and mail the coupon today!

Silhouette Intimate Moments®

Silhouette Books, 120 Brighton Rd., P.O. Box 5084, Clifton, NJ 07015-5084

READERS' COMMENTS ON SILHOUETTE DESIRES

"Thank you for Silhouette Desires. They are the best thing that has happened to the bookshelves in a long time."

—V.W.*, Knoxville, TN

"Silhouette Desires—wonderful, fantastic—the best romance around."

—H.T.*, Margate, N.J.

"As a writer as well as a reader of romantic fiction, I found DESIREs most refreshingly realistic—and definitely as magical as the love captured on their pages."

—C.M.*, Silver Lake, N.Y.

"I just wanted to let you know how very much I enjoy your Silhouette Desire books. I read other romances, and I must say your books rate up at the top of the list."

—C.N.*, Anaheim, CA

"Desires are number one. I especially enjoy the endings because they just don't leave you with a kiss or embrace; they finish the story. Thank you for giving me such reading pleasure."

—M.S.*, Sandford, FL

*names available on request